FESTIVALS, FEARS AND FATALITIES

THE JANE AUSTEN TEAROOM MYSTERIES
BOOK 2

SUZY BUSSELL

SNOWSHOES MEDIA

Festivals, Fears and Fatalities

The Jane Austen Tearoom Mysteries Book 2

By Suzy Bussell

This book has been written and edited using British English.

CHAPTER 1

I waved the last customer goodbye, turned the sign on the door to *Closed* and breathed a long sigh of relief. It was five o'clock in the afternoon, and I'd just finished clearing up after a long day in my Jane Austen-themed tearoom, in the Regency seaside town of Sidmouth in Devon.

My feet ached and I was hot and flustered. Wearing a Regency costume all day wasn't as comfortable as I'd imagined.

It was good that my tearoom was busy and I hadn't stopped all day. But still, I couldn't help feeling I'd bitten off more than I could chew.

My tearoom sat between two hotels in a distinctive Regency-style building on the esplanade, facing the sea. I shouldn't have been surprised that I was popular. Sidmouth is a busy seaside resort, and has been since 1795 when the Prince Regent visited, making it a popular resort for the upper and middle classes ever since.

It was decorated to sweep visitors into the charm of the Regency era. I had picked soft hues of cream and green throughout, with crisp white tablecloths edged in delicate lace. High-backed chairs, upholstered in period-appropriate patterns, circled the tables. Artworks, reminiscent of Jane Austen's narratives, were hung on the walls, enhancing the room's historical feel.

I looked at my watch. I had an hour to change out of my Regency dress and get to the Methodist Church hall for a very important meeting.

"Anything else you'd like me to do before I go?"

It was Carole, my full-time staff member. She was in her sixties and loved playing the part of Mrs Bennet to amuse the customers, including having a fit of the vapours. Like me, she also wore Regency-style clothes in the tearoom to add to the customer experience.

I'd recently taken on the persona of Mrs. Gardiner, Elizabeth Bennet's sensible and intelligent aunt, who often gives her niece sound advice. It didn't require much acting, but it meant that Carole and I could improvise conversations where Mrs Gardiner tries to calm Mrs Bennet.

However, to be taken seriously at the meeting tonight, I needed to get changed. My costume was fine in the tearoom, but I preferred to wear my own clothes when not working.

I'd opened my tearoom two months ago, and the opening ceremony had been the talk of Sidmouth – for all the wrong reasons. All the local dignitaries had come, and it had been a day to remember because Clive, head of the Sidmouth Business Consortium, had been murdered in the tearoom's garden.

Luckily, the murderer had been found. Well, actually, I'd discovered the murderer and had a lucky escape, thanks to my five strange new friends.

I glanced towards the other side of the tearoom. Standing in the small gift section were five ghosts.

That's right, five ghosts.

Someone – I still had no idea who – had dropped a magical turquoise ring through my letterbox. I believed it had been owned by the real Jane Austen, and when I put the ring on, I saw five ghosts with familiar-sounding names: Lily Barratt, Mr Wickers, Mr Collingwood, Mr Darby, and Lady Camilla Du Borg. They had inspired some of the characters in *Pride and Prejudice.*

I went over to them. "Do you want to come to the meeting or not?" I asked in a quiet voice so Carole couldn't hear.

"I do!" Lily said immediately.

I laughed. "You always want to go everywhere." Lily was a true adventurer. Maybe it was her age. She'd been fifteen when she'd died, and despite being a ghost for over two hundred years, didn't seemed to have grown up.

Mr Darby sighed. "Must we?" he said, in a severe tone.

Lily screwed up her nose. "You can hide and sulk if you like, but I'm going."

"Lady Camilla?"

Lady Camilla was peering out of the window. At the sound of her name, she turned. "I have no objection to attending."

"Mr Collingwood?"

As usual, he was standing slightly behind Lady Camilla, like her shadow. "I am happy to attend if Her Ladyship is." That was no surprise.

"Right then. I'll wear the ring. If you don't like it, just fall asleep or something."

"What about me?" Mr Wickers asked, in an indignant tone. He stood tall in his red military coat, white breeches, and long black boots. He was rather dashing, but I'd never feed his ego and tell him that.

"Sorry I missed you out, Mr Wickers. However, even if you don't want to go, you're outnumbered."

I didn't wait for an answer. Trying to please five ghosts with very different personalities was tricky, if not impossible, much of the time.

CHAPTER 2

quickly changed, then made my way the short distance to the Methodist Church hall in Sidmouth High Street. The meeting room was below street level, underneath the church. It was a building I was familiar with on the outside: It featured a traditional stone façade with arched windows and a prominent cross, but was complemented by a sleek and welcoming glass-fronted entrance.

As I went in, my heart thudded. I took a deep breath, hoping to steady the fluttering in my stomach. I wasn't sure why I was reacting like this. I'd done my fair share of volunteering at my son Oliver's school, mostly as part of the PTA. If they needed someone to do something, I had stepped up. That meant I was used to committee meetings, as well as doing all the dog's-body jobs no one else fancied. I had made myself so useful that when Oliver left school at sixteen to go to college, the school had begged me to stay on.

But this was completely different. The folk festival was the highlight of Sidmouth's calendar. People came from all over the country – all over the *world* – to attend.

To be quite honest, I could have done without the pressure of getting involved with the folk festival on top of running a new tearoom and making it a success. But I wanted to make a good impression in the town and this would help. I envisioned myself becoming a modern-day version of Anne Preston in Sidmouth. Anne was a much-loved stalwart of the town, and I admitted it to myself: I wanted to be admired just like her.

Everyone would know me. Everyone would have nothing but good to say about me, because I would help everyone and anyone. All I had to do was keep my opinions to myself, because my opinions had got me into trouble several times with the headmaster and the governors of Oliver's school.

My role on the folk festival committee was café and restaurant liaison, and from what I could tell, the majority of the work had already been done. I was taking over because James Pritchard, owner of the Coastal Crust pizza restaurant and takeaway, was in hospital after an accident. So when I was asked to help, I couldn't exactly say no. And in any case, I didn't want to. This was my stepping stone to greater things.

When I arrived with ghosts in tow, the other committee members, six of them, had already arrived and taken their seats around the table. The room itself had that musty church-hall smell, faintly damp and lingering. The walls were lined with dark wood panelling that made the space feel smaller than it was, as if the room were closing in on itself. The lighting was stark, with two fluorescent strip lights that gave the room an artificial glow, and highlighted the carpet which looked as though it had been installed in the seventies: muted browns and oranges in an odd geometric pattern, worn thin in spots. The atmosphere was heavy, almost oppressive. I couldn't help but notice how the committee member's expressions ranged from indifferent to mildly disapproving. I felt a knot tighten in my stomach. These people didn't seem warm or welcoming. They were judging me, and I wasn't quite sure how I'd measure up.

The ghosts had already spread out and were inspecting

the room. Lady Camilla's face had a distinct frown; it was not the sort of place she approved of.

I knew only one person, Laura. She was the one who'd come into my tearoom and roped me into the committee. She worked full time on the festival, and lived in Sidmouth, so she was a familiar face around the town and had come into the tearoom a few times. I realised in hindsight it was probably to size me up before she asked me to join the committee. She was dressed smart-casual, with black jeans and grey top. It made her look stylish, especially with a well-made-up face and dyed hair that kept her looking youthful.

Laura stood up when she saw me. "Hello, Trinity. Come and sit next to me."

I managed a nervous smile, then inched round the table and sat down beside Laura.

"Everyone, this is Trinity. I'll introduce you all properly later, but Trinity has kindly agreed to take over as café and restaurant liaison while James recovers from his injury."

The other committee members sniggered. Had I missed something?

Laura, seeing my confusion, whispered in my ear: "He got drunk and fell down the steps at Jacob's Ladder. Don't let on to him that I told you."

I heard a shriek of laughter. Lily had sneaked up behind me and listened in. I wanted to shoo her away, but I hadn't yet found a way of communicating with the ghosts when other people were in the room.

"Hush, girl," Lady Camilla scolded. Then she narrowed her eyes. "This room is shabby." Then she floated through a wall.

"Well, I'll introduce myself. I'm Martin Hawthorne, director of the folk festival. I've been doing this for twenty years now."

I smiled at Martin. I knew of him. Everyone did. He'd been one of two singers in Velvet Vortex, a well-known pop group in the eighties. They'd had a few number-one hits, made the cover of some teen magazines, then broken up, never to be heard of again. I remembered a few months back, there had been an eighties' revival concert in Exeter, with lots of bands performing their hits. Not tribute bands, the real ones. I was sure Velvet Vortex hadn't been listed on the poster I'd seen advertising it.

Martin had grey hair now, and lines on his face, but he was still good looking, and recognisable as an older version of the performer he'd been. He had a certain je ne sais quoi about him: an easy confidence.

I refocused on the present day as Martin continued talking. "There's not much for you to do at this stage, but we still need someone to be the contact point for the cafés and restaurants. Laura has a contact list for most of the eateries in the town, and I believe there's a phone messaging group?"

Laura nodded. "I'll give you all the details at the end of the meeting, Trinity."

That sounded fairly simple. A phone messaging group was easy. I could fit that into my schedule. I tried not to get too excited about helping with the festival.

Martin faced the room. "Right. On with the agenda. First of all, with three days until the start of the festival, the forecast says the weather will be dry and hot for the whole eight days. Which is excellent news."

He turned to the woman on his right. "Sarah, how's everything going with the campsite?" He turned back to me. "Sarah is the festival coordinator."

Sarah was in her late forties and radiated a no-nonsense vibe. She was in a plain white T-shirt, no make-up, and no jewellery.

Mr. Wickers floated up to Sarah and inspected her face. Sarah remained oblivious to his interest. "She doesn't like Martin." He caught my eye, and I raised an eyebrow. It was all I could do. I was dying to say something, but couldn't because of the others in the room. "There's definitely anger coming from her. I can't put my finger on why, but we'll see."

"Everything is going to plan," said Sarah. "The marquees are set up; the volunteers start arriving for their one-day training tomorrow. It's going uncannily well."

"Excellent, excellent," Martin said, leaning back in his chair.

The door opened, and a man stepped in. He was tall and slim, and his tight-fitting white T-shirt hugged his body. Silver hair framed his face in artfully tousled waves, and he wore dark sunglasses. He seemed effortlessly cool, with a trace of the rock star charisma.

I hadn't realised anyone else was expected, and judging by the look now on Martin's face, neither had he.

Martin's previous calm and welcoming expression twisted into something else entirely. His jaw tightened, his eyes gave a mix of irritation and unease.

"Hello, Martin," he drawled, his voice rich and smooth. He looked familiar, and after a moment, I recognised him.

Everybody watched him approach the table, his eyes fixed on Martin. "Long time no see."

CHAPTER 3

Martin shifted in his seat nervously. "What the—"

"Surprised to see me?" the man asked.

"Yes, I am. What are you doing here?"

A faint buzz of noise rose as the rest of us took in what was happening.

Lady Camilla floated back through the wall. "What is this hullabaloo all about?"

Mr Wickers crossed his arms and had a smirk on his face. "It's all about to 'kick off' as these modern people say."

"Is that who I think it is?" I whispered to Laura.

The man must have heard, because he turned to me. "Yes. I'm Danny Vance. I don't think we've had the pleasure of meeting before?" He flashed me a suggestive smile. I didn't know how to react.

Danny Vance, the other member of Velvet Vortex. This was no coincidence.

"What are you doing here?" Martin snapped.

"I came to help," Danny said smoothly.

Martin gave a nervous laugh.

Danny went to the side of the room, grabbed a plastic chair, and carried it to the table. "Budge up," he said. Two people reluctantly shuffled their chairs sideways, giving Danny just about enough room to get his chair in.

Martin managed to compose himself. "This is a damn imposition, Danny. Who do you think you are, coming in here? This is a private meeting, and you're not invited."

"That's not much of a welcome," Danny replied. "However, I have been invited. Your colleague Sarah has asked me to join the committee."

All heads turned towards Sarah, who flushed bright red.

Martin's eyes narrowed. "What?"

I realised my mouth had dropped open and closed it.

"Oh dear," said Mr Darby to Lady Camilla, who was listening with keen interest. "I suspect that this will not end well." He folded his arms.

Mr Wickers rubbed his hands together. "It's hotting up." Even Mr Collingwood was floating closer.

Sarah's flush deepened. "Danny was the reason that Merrydown Way agreed to headline the festival."

Danny leaned back in his chair. "Yup, I was the one who persuaded the hottest folk band in Europe to schlep all the way down to Sidmouth to play the festival. Without me, you wouldn't have one of the most famous bands with mass appeal, mixing pop, rock, and folk, at the top of the bill."

"Oh, I've heard of them!" Lily said, excitedly. "Trinity, your neighbour was playing their music the other night. And the night before that. And the night before that."

Lily must have been in my neighbour's house. I wasn't sure if I was upset or amused at that. Either way, there was nothing I could do to stop her.

Most people had heard of Merrydown Way. Non-ghosts, anyway. They had a distinctive sound, and had been successful for many years, with several hit albums. A one-hit wonder they were not.

Martin huffed. "How do *you* know *them*, let alone have any influence over where they choose to play?"

"Well, Martin, I haven't been idle since you threw me out of the band all those years ago."

"Are you saying that *I* broke up the band? No, you did that all by yourself."

Danny rolled his eyes. "Still in denial, I see," he said, shaking his head. "Unfortunately, Martin here can't tell the difference between the actual truth, and his truth."

Martin stood up and pointed to the door. "Get out!"

Danny smiled, folded his arms, then stretched out his legs under the table. "Nope. I'm here to help, Martin, and help I will. From what I've heard lately, you need all the help you can get."

Martin turned to Sarah. "This is your fault. What do you think you were doing, inviting him to join the committee? You had no right."

Sarah bristled. "I put out feelers in the industry and Danny responded. Simple as that. And as it happens, he's had some other great ideas, as well as persuading Merrydown Way to headline for us."

It was Martin's turn to flush. "I could have booked a band just as good as Merrydown Way, if not better."

Sarah's eyebrows shot up. "Oh, really? As I recall, you got me to try and book Wandering Yew, but they wouldn't come. Not even when I name-dropped you. Said it was too small for them. I tried other bands, too, but they all said they wouldn't do it because of what happened last year."

The room went absolutely silent, and everyone except Sarah studied the table.

I cleared my throat. Someone had to ask; it might as well be me. "What happened last year?"

Martin sighed deeply and rubbed his temples. "Last year... Well, it was a disaster. Hazel & The Hearth were the headline act. Everything was set up for what was supposed to be the highlight of the festival. Then the weather took a turn for the worse. A freak summer storm hit, and our equipment wasn't good enough to handle it. We lost power halfway through the band's set, and the whole place was flooded. Their instruments were damaged, the sound system was ruined, and we couldn't get things back up and running."

"It wasn't just the technical issues," said Sarah. "The band were furious and their management threatened to sue. Word spreads quickly in the industry. Now, no one wants to risk playing here. They think it's cursed or something."

I glanced around the table, seeing the mix of frustration and embarrassment on everyone's faces. "So, you're saying that Merrydown Way agreed to play despite this?"

"Yes," said Sarah. "But it took a lot of convincing, as well as promises that we've upgraded all our equipment and have contingency plans in place for any weather conditions."

"Let's just hope it's enough," Martin muttered.

The room fell silent again, the weight of last year's failure hanging in the air.

It was Mr Darby who broke the silence, for me, anyway: no one else could hear him. "I think Mr Vance has done a commendable thing by persuading Merrydown Way to play."

"I do, too," I said, out loud. Talking to the ghosts had become second nature, but it was always a bit tricky around others. I felt that familiar wave of self-consciousness, but thankfully, everyone just assumed I was talking to Martin.

Outside the church hall, half an hour later, when the meeting had finished, I contemplated that although I knew helping out at the folk festival would be stressful, I hadn't been expecting this type of stress.

CHAPTER 4

The following week I had been mega-busy in the tearoom and answering festival queries. There was more to the job than Laura had said. It seemed the restaurant owners and street food eateries had lots of questions about the festival and how it would impact their businesses. Many of them also needed more temporary staff over the festival period, and wanted advice on how to get them. That left me questioning whether I should have recruited some myself. My days were filled with serving tea and scones, followed by answering questions from the restaurant and café owners.

I woke early the next morning, and decided to go for a brisk walk along the seafront before heading to the tearoom.

I'd recently listened to a podcast which said that an early morning walk helps you wake up and stay healthy. Although I was on my feet in the tearoom all day, I also wanted to get some fresh sea air. Since I had moved back to Sidmouth from London, I was enjoying being by the sea more and more. When I'd grown up there, I hadn't appreciated being by the seaside. Now I was in my early forties, I realised how lucky I was to be living on the coast. I preferred the smell of the sea to exhaust fumes.

It didn't take any persuasion to have the ghosts with me. Only Mr Darby was reluctant, stating that he'd rather stay and watch TV. But he was outvoted by the others.

As Martin had said in the meeting the week before, the weather was good, with a very gentle breeze coming in from the English Channel. There weren't many people around, as it was very early: just a few dog walkers on the esplanade.

Rows of market stalls had been constructed on the seafront, bunting was strung up everywhere, and a wave of expectation rushed over me. My tearoom would be busy, I was sure of it, and I hoped the extra income from the festival goers would help to pay off some of the tearoom's setup costs.

I reached the other end of the esplanade, where the River Sid flowed into the English Channel. Then I walked inland to an area called the Ham and the main festival marquee, which housed a large stage and seating for five hundred people. The white tent covered the entire area next to the river. It was the centre piece of the festival. Therefore, I mused, it was also where last year's disaster had happened. Hopefully, this year, everything would be perfect.

I walked towards the ticket office, a temporary kiosk placed near the entrance. Just a few days to go now.

I remembered the festival from my youth: it had brought the town to life. Although I hadn't really been into the music, it had a really good vibe. And all the restaurant and café owners I had spoken to over the last week had said they earned enough money during the folk festival to keep them going for the rest of the year. I could hardly wait.

I passed the ticket kiosk, glancing over my shoulder to check for traffic, when Lily's scream cut through the morning air.

I jolted, spinning around. "Lily, what's wrong?"

She was hovering by the kiosk, hands clamped over her mouth, eyes wide with shock. The other ghosts flocked toward her, all of them staring inside. Lily pointed, her hand trembling, toward the interior.

"What is it?" My heart raced as I moved closer, peering through the window.

And then I saw him.

Martin slumped in his chair, head tilted at an unnatural angle, his eyes vacant and half-lidded. His skin had a pale pallor, lifeless. My breath caught in my throat.

Martin was dead.

CHAPTER 5

tried not to panic. Thoughts rushed through my head – what should I do first? Then the ghosts crowded round me.

"Oh dear!" Lady Camilla folded her arms. "Oh dear me. That gentleman is deceased."

Mr Darby peered at him through the wall of the kiosk for a moment. "That's the gentleman who was running the meeting last week."

"Now, Trinity, remember to breathe," Mr Wickers said. He came close to me, then gasped for air whilst moving his arms as if he were conducting an orchestra. "Come on. Breathe in … and out…"

I didn't know what to say. I stared at Martin.

"Are you sure he's dead?" I asked the ghosts.

"I didn't scream for the fun of it," Lily complained.

I let out a sigh. "I didn't think you did. Just that you might have been mistaken."

She shook her head.

Mr Darby went fully through the wall of the kiosk this time and inspected Martin's body. "He has a wound on his head. I'd wager it was murder and that is how the killer did it. There is nothing in the kiosk that could have caused such a wound accidentally."

I shivered.

"The door to the kiosk is unlocked," Mr Darby stated.

"So he was killed here?" I asked.

"I believe that to be the case." Mr Darby floated back out.

"Can you sense his spirit?" I asked the ghosts.

They all looked very serious, then shook their heads. "This gentleman has departed to the afterlife," Mr Collingwood said reverently.

"Now, then, young lady," said Lady Camilla briskly, "you need to call the police."

"Oh, yes. Yes I do." I took my phone out of my bag and went to dial 999. Then I thought it might be better to phone DI Cormac O'Malley directly. DI O'Malley was a local detective I'd got to know after the unfortunate murder in my tearoom. He'd been the investigating officer.

My hands trembled as I pressed the buttons. He answered after a few rings. "Hel-*lo* there." His Irish accent always sounded stronger over the phone. "Bit early for a call. Are you all right? Not discovered a dead body or anything?"

"I-I…"

"Trinity…?"

"Actually … I have just found a dead body."

DI O'Malley let out a nervous laugh. "Are you joking with me?"

"No, I'm really not. It's Martin Hawthorne, the director of the folk festival. He's dead, and from the looks of it, it's murder."

"Where are you?"

"At the Ham. By the ticket booth at the main marquee, by the river."

"Stay there. I'm leaving now." The phone call ended.

I looked at my phone, then at the ghosts. They were floating above Martin, examining his body.

"Looks like whatever stuck him was very hard. Metal, I'd warrant," Mr Darby commented.

"I agree," said Mr Collingwood.

Lady Camilla tossed her head and huffed. "What sort of place is this town, now? Not one, but TWO murders in the space of weeks." She glared at me.

"It isn't my fault!" I cried. "I haven't murdered anyone, and Devon has one of the lowest crime rates in the UK."

"Not any more, it hasn't," Lady Camilla said in disgust.

She had a point. All I could do now was wait for O'Malley.

CHAPTER 6

paced, wondering how long I would have to wait. I knew that O'Malley lived in Exmouth. It would take him at least twenty minutes to get to Sidmouth. And that didn't take rush hour into account. I imagined him sitting in traffic, drumming on the steering wheel and huffing. Even worse, if the traffic was clear, he could get stuck behind a tractor. They were always clogging up the roads. I shook myself. I shouldn't be complaining about farm vehicles. Devon was a farming county, and I needed to stop thinking like a Londoner.

"Keep a lookout, will you?" I asked Lily. She floated up into the sky, keeping watch.

A few minutes later, a police car pulled up. However, it wasn't O'Malley, but two uniformed officers. O'Malley must have called the station. And one of the officers was my cousin Francis.

Francis was in his early thirties, the only son of my Aunt Ruby. He'd been a police officer for about a year, so he was still very new in the job. He clapped his police hat on his head and stumbled slightly as he rushed to me.

"You found a body?" he gasped.

"Yes. He's over there in the ticket kiosk. It's Martin Hawthorne; he's head of the folk festival."

Francis flung out his arms. "Stay back, please."

"I haven't touched anything."

"We'll have to cordon off the area."

"Aren't you going to take a look at him?" I pointed towards the ticket booth.

"Er…" Francis looked over. "No. No, I'm not. I don't need to see anything. Not my job."

I raised an eyebrow. "Are you scared of seeing a dead body?"

"No!" he snapped, scowling at me.

Mr Wickers grinned. "He's definitely scared."

The other officer, a woman who looked ridiculously young, got out of the driver's side of the car and came over. The scared look left Francis's face, and he almost stood to attention as she approached.

"Good morning," she said, her tone calm but professional. "I'm PC Sutton." She gave me a quick but earnest look. "You must be Trinity, yes?"

I nodded, feeling the tension in my shoulders ease at the officer's reassuring demeanor.

PC Sutton gave me gentle smile. "Are you all right? I know it's been a shock, so if you need to sit down or take a minute, just let me know."

I managed a small smile in return, grateful for the kindness. "Thank you. I'm okay. He's in the ticket booth," I told her, and she went in to look. I wanted to follow, but I didn't want to risk any further contamination of the crime scene.

She reappeared after a short time. "It's a dead body, for sure." She turned to my cousin. "Francis – I mean PC Bishop – we need to make sure the crime scene is preserved. If you could fetch the tape and place some from there to there…" She pointed to indicate where she meant.

Francis nodded eagerly and ran to the police car to collect the tape.

He emerged a minute later, arms overflowing with different items: tape, a camera case, a sign that read *POLICE INCIDENT* and some metal stakes, presumably to hold the tape in place.

Lily whizzed down from her lookout post, practically vibrating with excitement as she floated in front of me, her eyes wide. "DI Handsome is here! I can see his car. He'll come around the corner any moment!"

My stomach did an unexpected flip, and I felt my cheeks heat up despite myself and the situation. I had to play it cool.

Thirty seconds later, DI O'Malley's black Ford Mondeo pulled up behind the police car and he got out. He wore a jacket over a shirt with the sleeves rolled up, his short dark hair a bit tousled, like he hadn't spared a thought for it. Clearly, he was here to get straight to work, not to fuss over appearances.

PC Sutton went straight up to him. "We're cordoning off the area, sir. I called an ambulance, and its on the way to confirm the death, and the woman who found the body is waiting there to give a statement."

I looked over to see Francis wrestling with the police tape, which twisted and knotted around his arms. He gripped a stake and tried to push it into the ground, but it wobbled unsteadily, slipping from his hand before he managed to plant it firmly. He stooped to grab it again, nearly tangling himself in the tape in the process.

O'Malley nodded and glanced in my direction. I met his eyes and managed a sheepish smile.

"Okay, thanks. PC Sutton, can you do me a favour?"

She nodded enthusiastically. "Of course, sir."

"Can you update the station and get them to call forensics? I'll take it from here."

"Yes sir." She beamed at O'Malley, then went to the police car.

O'Malley watched her walk away, then came over to me. "How are you, Trinity?" he murmured, and put his hand on my arm. I felt a spark of electricity go through me. I looked into his dark eyes and felt that familiar hypnotic pull.

"I-I'm all right. A bit shocked, but better than poor Martin."

"Where is he?"

"In the ticket booth."

He let his hand drop. "And when did you find him?"

"Just before I called you. A minute or so before, maybe. It took me a little while to pull myself together."

He took two blue plastic shoe coverings from his pocket and placed them over his feet. "Do you know him at all?"

"I know *of* him, really. I've only met him once, and that was last week. He's Martin Hawthorne, the director of the folk festival."

He nodded. "Did you touch anything?"

"No. I just looked in through the window."

"Right, I'll take a look." He strode off and disappeared around the corner of the kiosk.

Lily floated behind him, pausing by the side of it. "He's examining the body."

"Yes. He said," I murmured.

"He's checking he's dead." Lily paused. "Now he's taking some photos with his phone."

DI O'Malley reappeared after a few minutes, a deep frown on his face. "You said you met him for the first time last week?"

"Yes. I've been roped into the festival committee."

"Doing what?"

"I'm the café and restaurant liaison."

He nodded.

"The folk festival committee want to make sure the café

and restaurant owners and staff are kept up to date with everything," I gabbled. I wasn't sure why I'd even said that, unless it was to break the silence.

"That's understandable, given the huge amount of tourists who come for the festival." He thought for a moment. "So, when you met him last week, how did he seem to you?"

I took a deep breath, wondering how to put it, then sighed it out: "Well, to be honest, it was a bit tense."

His frown deepened. "How so?"

"I thought the folk festival would have a harmonious, efficient committee who all got on together. That's what I was expecting, anyway."

"But it wasn't like that?"

"No! I got the impression that most of them didn't even like each other. To top things off, Martin's ex-bandmate turned up last night, too, and they had a row."

"His ex-bandmate? Martin was in a band?"

"Yes, Velvet Vortex. They were big in the eighties."

O'Malley frowned. "The name rings a bell."

"You've probably heard their songs on the radio. They get played a lot on the smaller radio stations these days as they are decades old."

He half smiled. "I'll take your word for it."

"Maybe they never became famous in Ireland."

"Perhaps not." He mused for a moment. "Okay, so this bandmate that turned up – do you know his name?"

"Yes. Danny Vance."

"And what were they arguing about?"

"Danny had persuaded a top band to be the headline act for the folk festival."

"But surely that's good?"

"Yes, but Martin wasn't told about Danny's involvement. And from what they both said, Velvet Vortex broke up acrimoniously. Martin wasn't happy to see Danny at all. And

Danny knew he wouldn't be: seemed to like the fact he's annoyed Martin simply for being around."

"Thank you, that's a great help. I'll need you to give me a list of all the other people who were at the meeting last week." He handed me his notebook and a pen, and I wrote down the names of everyone who had been there.

"I don't know their full names, but Sarah can tell you if you contact her first. She has the minutes to the meetings."

An unmarked white transit van pulled up, and three people got out, dressed in white overalls.

O'Malley glanced over. "Ah, forensics are here. I'll need to speak to them." He returned his attention to me. "Are you quite sure you're all right, Trinity? I'll ask you to give a proper statement down at the station later, but now you can go. I guess you'll need to go and open up the tearoom?"

I looked at my watch. It was already quarter past eight. "Yes, you're right. In fact, I'm interviewing someone for a job there in half an hour." I could feel myself tensing up. "I'd better go and get ready for them."

CHAPTER 7

I left O'Malley with the forensics team and made my way along the esplanade to my tearoom in a sort of daze. My morning walk hadn't been the relaxing experience I was expecting, and now I regretted taking it in the first place.

Poor Martin. When I'd got home from the meeting last week, I'd realised that I didn't like him very much. He had seemed a bit overconfident and possibly slapdash. But some of the other committee members should take some of the flack if he was just a figurehead. Anyway, he hadn't deserved to be murdered.

Before I changed into my costume, I started to get out the cakes and scones and lay out cutlery and crockery. Before I knew it, it was time for the interview with my prospective new tearoom employee.

At first, Carole and Emma had been all the staff I needed, but now it was becoming clear that I needed at least one more employee as backup, and to help over the busy summer period.

I was determined to have a man who could take on a well-known Austen character and add extra variety.

Only one man had applied for the position, though, so I

hoped he'd be suitable. In his personal statement, Alan had said that he wanted a job to liven up his retirement. If he was up to it, he could be Mr Bennet, Mr Woodhouse, or if he was feeling particularly nasty that day, Colonel Tilney.

Alan arrived exactly on time, as I expected he would. According to his CV, he was sixty-eight and had worked as an accountant for most of his life. He was tall and well-built, with broad shoulders and a sturdy frame that suggested he hadn't spent all his time behind a desk. His silver hair was impeccably styled, and he wore a neatly trimmed beard that added to his air of quiet authority. His posture was straight, almost military.

There was something about his presence that made you want to stand a little straighter, out of respect.

"Hello! Do come in and sit down." We shook hands, then I indicated a table by the window, and we sat opposite each other.

We regarded one another for a moment. I couldn't help wondering why a man like Alan, a retired accountant, would want to work in a tearoom.

As Alan settled into his seat, I could sense the familiar presence of the ghosts. Lily appeared first, hovering nearby, her expression curious and faintly amused. "He seems very proper," she murmured, tilting her head.

"So, I imagine you're interested in knowing why I want to work in the tearoom?" he asked.

"Er, yes." How strange. I had actually been thinking that. Although, it was an obvious question for an interview.

"Well, I'm looking for a part-time job that will get me out of the house and keep me physically active. And meeting people, of course. I love meeting people and talking."

"And you used to work as an accountant?"

"That's right."

Mr. Darby floated close by, adjusting his cravat. "I'd say he's got the bearing of a military man rather than an accountant. Look at that posture. Straight as a ramrod." He sniffed.

An accountant: that might be helpful if I got stuck while I was doing my own books. I felt sure Alan wouldn't mind giving me some advice.

"I don't mind helping out with your accounts, if you need it. But I'd prefer to work mainly in the tearoom."

I couldn't help staring at him. He seemed to know exactly what I was going to ask.

Lady Camilla tilted her head; she studied Alan intently. "There's something remarkable about this man," she said, her voice low and thoughtful. "Do you feel it, Collingwood? It's as though he's ... connected to something deeper."

Mr Collingwood approached. "You are indeed correct, madam. He has tuned into Trinity's thoughts. But I don't sense anything malicious. If anything, it feels like he wants to help. It's rare to meet someone with such a strong sense of integrity."

I wasn't sure what to think about that so I asked my next question. "So, from your CV, you don't have any experience working in a café or restaurant?"

"Only voluntarily. I used to help run the Memory Café in my old town. Just a drop-in, for carers and those with Alzheimer's, but people can be picky about their tea and coffee, and I'm good at learning things. Despite my age."

This all sounded great. Hopefully, he wouldn't mind putting on a costume for the job—

"Oh, and I'll be fine wearing a Regency costume. I've read all Jane Austen's books, and I was thinking I could alternate between Mr Bennet and Mr Woodhouse."

"He has all the makings of a Mr. Bennet: charming, intelligent, and just the right age. He'd fit perfectly," Lady Camilla stated.

I managed to smile, even though I was slightly unnerved, not at Lady Camilla's comment, but at the fact Alan was actually pre-empting my questions now. Then again, I supposed that my questions were on the obvious side, since I ran an Austen-themed tearoom.

"Which is your favourite Austen b—"

"*Persuasion.*" Alan smiled at me. He reminded me of a favourite uncle who you might not see very often, but who always showed an interest in how you were and what you were doing.

Lily huffed. "Shame it's not *Pride and Prejudice.*"

I felt both happy and relieved. Alan seemed like a nice man, and it would be good to have an extra hand around the place.

"How soon can you start?" It wasn't long before Alan would be needed, what with the folk festival starting in less than a week.

"The day after tomorrow?"

"Perfect. I don't have a Regency costume for you yet, obviously, as you'll need to be measured. Just wear something smart."

"Oh, I have my own Regency costume. I'll wear that."

My eyebrows shot up. "You do?"

"My late wife used to love going to the Jane Austen festival in Bath, and I'd accompany her."

"Oh, I see. I'm sorry for your loss."

"Thank you." He looked around the tearoom wistfully. "She would have loved it here."

The silence grew. I wasn't sure what else to say.

Alan stood up. "Well, I'll come the day after tomorrow morning, and you can train me up. I can only do two days a week, apart from the folk festival. I expect you'll want me to work more hours when that's on."

I stood up, too. "Yes, I will." I smiled. "Welcome on board."

"An excellent choice of servant," Lady Camilla stated as we all watched Alan leave the tearoom.

"Thank you," I replied. "Not that there was much choice."

"I will reserve judgement until I see him in costume," Mr Darby stated.

I turned to Mr Collingwood. "What did you mean when you said he had tuned into my thoughts? Is he a mind reader?" I gave a small laugh. Then I stopped myself when I saw Mr Collingwood's expression.

"Indeed, madam. Certain humans have a particular ability to sense others' thoughts. I have seen it a few times over the years—"

Lady Camilla interrupted him, "Yes, he is one of them. I am sure of it. Some use it for evil, but that man… No, he was not using it maliciously. Besides, they can't read minds, only get strong feelings."

"Like an empath?"

Lady Camilla nodded. "Yes, but they can influence feelings, too. In Alan's case, for the good."

First ghosts, now mind readers. I wondered what other spectral surprises lay in wait for me.

CHAPTER 8

As soon as Alan had left, a dark cloud seemed to settle over me. I was pleased that he could start the day after tomorrow, and it would be much better to have another person working in the tearoom, to relieve some of the pressure. But my mind kept replaying the moment when I had seen Martin sprawled lifeless in the ticket office.

I busied myself in the kitchen until half an hour later Mr Collingwood floated in. "I do beg your pardon, madam, but your policeman by the name of O'Malley is at the front door."

"Thank you, Mr Collingwood. It's very kind of you to tell me."

Mr Collingwood gave a deep bow, then dissipated.

I dried my hands, then made my way through the tearoom. O'Malley and I smiled at each other through the glass.

I unlocked the door. "Come in."

I wasn't sure why, but I always got a good feeling whenever O'Malley was around. I'd had a similar feeling when I interviewed Alan, but with O'Malley it was more intense.

"I'm just prepping for opening. Is it okay if we talk in the kitchen?"

"Yeah, sure. You carry on and I'll talk."

He followed me into the kitchen and watched me cut out scones. I put them on a baking tray, slid them into the oven, and set the timer. I wondered when he would start talking.

"How are you?" he asked.

"Checking up on me again? Or are you hungry?" I teased with a smile.

"Checking up on you. Finding a dead body, particularly a murdered dead body is never nice."

"So it's murder?" I knew already, thanks to the ghosts.

"It seems Martin Hawthorne was struck on the head with some kind of hammer. That's what would correspond to his head wound. So we're definitely treating it as murder."

"That's terrible."

"We're about to search his house to see if we find anything there, but I wanted to check you were all right first."

That gave me a quiet sense of satisfaction.

We were interrupted by Lily, who zoomed into the kitchen, looking fit to burst with news. "Sorry to interrupt, but your friend Holly is here."

"Oh," I said, before I could stop myself. Hopefully, O'Malley would think I was responding to him.

Holly had probably come because she'd heard about the murder. And my involvement. Again.

"I think my friend Holly is here, too." I went into the tearoom and let her in.

"Hello, my darling! Francis told me all about the body this morning. How shocking. You must be so upset." Holly was wearing denim dungarees, a pink T-shirt underneath and some Doc Martin boots.

O'Malley walked through from the kitchen.

Holly saw him and stopped. "Oh, hello. Are you here on police business, or just popping in to see Trin?"

I gave Holly a significant look. "He's here to give me an update."

"What happened?" she asked.

"I thought you said Francis told you?"

She waved a dismissive hand. "I want to hear it from the horse's mouth." She walked into the kitchen; O'Malley and I followed.

I shrugged. "I went for a quiet early morning walk down to the river and stumbled upon his dead body. In the festival ticket office."

Holly pulled up one of the high chairs and sat down. "How terrible for you, Trin. I can't believe there's been so much murder in our peaceful town lately. It must have been someone from outside the area. Nobody in this town would murder poor Martin. He was so well-liked."

"He was?" O'Malley and I said, together.

"Everyone I know who knows, knew him … said he was lovely."

Mr Darcy stepped forward and leaned down to my ear. "But someone disliked him so much that they murdered him."

"My thoughts exactly," I said out loud, and O'Malley gave me a puzzled look.

"Well, I'm sure you'll find the murderer, Trinity. Especially after last time. You seem to have a knack for detection." She gave O'Malley a sly smile. "How long had Martin been dead when he was found?"

"We'll know more when the postmortem report comes in." He turned to me. "Trinity, I need you to come into the station and give a formal statement. Can you come today?"

"Sure." I smiled, hoping that Holly would keep quiet and not ask any more questions. She was certainly more brazen in her questioning than I would be.

Holly's phone beeped a message had arrived. She looked at it, then sighed. "Got to go. Delivery at the shop. She jumped off the chair. "Are you sure you're all right, Trin? It's just that I need to go."

"I'm fine."

"Well, let me know if you need me, or when you've worked out who did it." She kissed me on the cheek, said goodbye to us both, and breezed out.

That left me alone with O'Malley again.

"I can come to the station after I close at four o'clock."

"Thanks."

I expected O'Malley to make a move to leave, but he stayed put. I checked the oven timer, then picked up a rolling pin and started rolling out another batch of scone dough.

"How did you find Martin's body?" he asked, suddenly. "He was inside the ticket booth, well out of sight."

I froze. Obviously, I couldn't tell him that a ghost had alerted me. I looked desperately at Lily for help. She'd been floating nearby, listening in as usual.

"Tell him you were walking around the ticket booth, admiring it," said Lily.

My eyebrows were halfway up my forehead, but I couldn't think of anything better. So I repeated what Lily had said.

He gave me a skeptical look. "Admiring the ticket booth?"

"Yes. They're very clever, aren't they? Portable, compact. What's not to like?"

He stared at me. Did he know I was lying? I was sure he did.

Lucky for me, his phone rang, breaking the spell, and he looked at the screen. "Sorry, I need to get this. I'll see you later at the station."

He answered the phone and walked out.

I put my hands on the counter and sighed out a breath. "Admiring the ticket booth?" I repeated to Lily. "Seriously?"

She shrugged, then giggled. "It was all I could think of."

"It was more than I could, I suppose. Though I don't think O'Malley believed me."

"Perhaps not," Lily replied. "His expression was very funny when you said it."

I sighed.

"Your friend Holly is a gossip," Lady Camilla said disapprovingly.

"Yes, she is. But that can come in handy sometimes, when you're trying to solve a murder."

Lady Camilla's eyes narrowed. "Are you going to try and solve another murder?"

I should have said no, but "Yes" came out of my mouth before I could stop myself.

Lily clapped her hands together excitedly, though it made no sound. "Good! That will give us all something to do."

Lady Camilla tutted at Lily.

"What?" Lily complained. "Don't pretend you don't relish trying to solve mysteries. It could be like the one in 1924, when—"

"Hush!" said Mr Darby, putting a finger to his lips. "We do not speak of past ring-owners, Lily. You know that."

"That's such a stupid rule," I said, annoyed that the ghosts wouldn't talk about past ring-owners and their escapades. "Can't you tell me some of it, without telling me who the ring-holder was?"

"No!" Mr Darby said. "Never!"

"Suit yourself," I said, and carried on rolling out scones as if I didn't care one bit. Although, of course, I did.

CHAPTER 9

At four o'clock sharp, I turned the sign to Closed, changed out of my Regency dress and into everyday clothes, and made my way to the police station, an old building on the way out of town which had served as the local station for at least a hundred years.

The police station was a modest two-story building. Its weathered stone façade had the marks of a century's worth of coastal winds and rain. The structure had a certain charm, with ivy creeping up one side, and tall, narrow windows framed by faded white trim. Inside, the atmosphere shifted from historical to practical, though the station still retained hints of its age.

The waiting room was small and functional with a small glass hatch which was closed and a blind pulled down. I pressed the button in front of the hatch but it made no sound. The worst kind of button. However, a moment later, the glass slid aside and a police officer stared back at me. He was at least sixty, with grey hair that had been cut a little too short to suit him. "How can I help?" he asked.

"I'm Trinity Bishop. I found the dead body – I mean, Martin Hawthorne – this morning. Cormac – I mean, DI

O'Malley – asked me to come in and give a statement." I felt myself blush as I said O'Malley's name and told myself off. I wasn't a teenager any more; I was forty-two. Too old to blush at the mention of a man I found attractive.

The police officer nodded. "I'll tell him you're here."

It didn't take long for the door to open and O'Malley to appear. He held the door open for me. "Come through," he said, with a smile. He looked a little rough around the edges. Stubble was present on his chin, and his eyes were bloodshot. It must have been a stressful few hours for him.

I stood up and followed him to an interview room.

"Would you like a cup of tea? It's nothing like as good as the tea you offer, but it would be rude of me not to ask."

I shook my head. "The thing about working in a tearoom is that you can drink as much tea as you like. I've already had more than enough today."

The interview room was plain, with a table in the middle and two chairs either side. This was obviously where they interviewed suspects, as well as witnesses like me. O'Malley gestured to a chair on one side of the table and I took it. I thought he would sit opposite me, but he sat in the chair beside mine. Then he got up. "I'll just fetch the paperwork." He disappeared.

Mr Wickers shuddered. "This place is giving me the heebie-jeebies." The ghosts had come with me of course. All crowded in the small interview room, it made it feel confined.

"That's a bit strange, coming from a ghost," I said.

"Shhh." He pointed to a CCTV camera in the corner ceiling. "You don't want DI Handsome thinking you're a crazy lady who talks to her imaginary friends."

I looked up at the camera, then at Mr Wickers. "It won't be switched on for me, will it?"

Mr Collingwood floated up and examined it. "It is currently on," he said, seriously. "Mr Wickers is correct; you must not speak to us. Unless you wish to appear unhinged."

I sighed. Hopefully O'Malley wouldn't watch it back. There was no reason for him to.

O'Malley returned a moment later with a folder which he placed on the table. "I'm a bit rusty. I usually get a detective sergeant to take these sorts of statements. But seeing as it's you, I thought I'd do it." He half smiled at me.

"I don't mind giving my statement to a sergeant, if that's easier," I said, hoping he wouldn't take me up on it. "You must have a lot to do, especially this early in the case."

"I do, but this is a welcome distraction."

"Do you have any idea when he was murdered?"

"The postmortem is happening even as we speak, but we think it was sometime late last night or very early this morning."

I stared at him. "What on earth was Martin doing in the ticket booth at that time?"

"That's what we're trying to find out. If we can work out Martin's last movements, we should be able to pinpoint who killed him. However, with the folk festival so imminent, he was busy doing all sorts of things."

I mused, "I'm not sure how much he had to do. Sarah seemed to do most of the work. She had a long to-do list at the committee meeting."

O'Malley nodded. "I'll check with her. All right, Trinity. Let's go through what happened this morning when you found Martin."

I hesitated for a moment, collecting my thoughts. "Well, I was walking along the esplanade, as I'd decided to go for an early morning walk. I didn't really have much appreciation of living by the sea in my youth, but after twenty years in London, I really appreciate it now. I decided to walk past the tearoom, and to the end of the esplanade, then have a look at the central festival area on the Ham. That's when I..." I faltered, the image of Martin's lifeless form flashing in my mind.

Lily came closer, her expression solemn. "Remember, you were drawn to the ticket booth: admiring its charm, weren't you?"

I didn't want to lie to O'Malley, but he'd never believe me if I told him a ghost had alerted me.

I nodded slightly, then spoke. "I don't know why, but I decided to look more closely at the ticket booth. It's such a quaint little thing, and I was struck by how clean and well-kept it was."

O'Malley had been typing my statement into the tablet computer he held. He stopped and glanced at me, raising an eyebrow, but said nothing, waiting for me to continue.

Lily whispered in my ear, "I saw him. I floated through the booth, thinking it would be empty. But there he was. Slumped over, not moving."

I swallowed, then continued. "I peered through the window. At first, I thought it was empty, but then I saw him. I could tell he was dead."

"You were so shocked, I had to tell you to phone the police," Lady Camilla reminded me.

"Then I called you."

"Did you see anyone suspicious?" O'Malley asked.

"No," I said firmly.

"All right, so read through it, and sign at the bottom." He handed me the tablet computer and an electronic pen.

I read through the statement and signed it.

O'Malley's phone beeped: a text message had arrived. He glanced at it and frowned.

"Is everything all right?" I ventured.

"Just my ex-wife."

It was the first time he'd mentioned her. Up until now, all I'd heard about her was from gossip.

"My ex-husband texts me sometimes. Usually about money. I wish he wouldn't. It's hard, isn't it?"

"You're telling me. She wants me to pick the kids up from

school tomorrow. That's tricky when I'm heading up a murder investigation."

I gave him a sympathetic look.

"One of the reasons we broke up was my working hours."

"That's understandable, though, when you're a police officer. Protecting the community comes at a price."

His dark, hypnotic eyes searched mine. "You're right. It does." He seemed relieved that someone understood the pressure he was under.

"I've always believed that the most meaningful things in life require sacrifices," I said. "Your dedication is admirable. But you have to remember to take care of yourself, too."

I let myself rest my hand on his arm, like he'd touched mine that morning.

Lady Camilla huffed. "Very forward for a young lady."

Lily sniggered.

Then the interview-room door burst open, and my cousin Francis poked his head around it. His eyes widened, and I pulled my hand away as if O'Malley's arm was red hot.

"Ooh, I do hope this isn't a bad time," said Francis, grinning.

O'Malley recovered first. "To what do we owe the pleasure, Constable Bishop?"

Francis didn't look at all put down. "Sorry to disturb you, sir, but DC Samuels needs you." He gave me a little wave. "Hi, Trin."

I gave him a small wave.

O'Malley got up. "Sorry, I've got to go. I'll see you out."

We parted company at the door of the police station and I set off for home.

I was bursting to have a proper conversation with the ghosts.

"We need to find out Martin's movements during his last few hours," said Mr. Wickers, rubbing his chin as he went.

"I'll speak to the committee members and try to find out if any of them spent time with Martin last night," I said.

"Excellent," Mr Wickers agreed.

When I got home, I put on a pan of pasta. As I watched it simmer away, I checked my phone.

The message group for the local restaurant and café owners showed eighty-six unread messages. I sighed and scrolled through.

Is it true about Martin? said Helen, the owner of the tapas bar.

Yes, replied Mike from the fish and chip shop on the front.

OMG I can't believe it!

Do we know why/how?

Anne from the Donkey charity shop said it was murder. Police were there. Must be serious.

And it went on like that. Until I saw the owner of a café ask:

Did anyone see Martin last night?

The next message was from Fred at the Swan Inn. *I did. He came into the bar with Jazz and they had a drink. It was late, ten thirty, and I had to kick them out at eleven.*

I mused on this new information. Martin had gone out after the committee meeting with someone called Jazz. An interesting name for someone at a folk festival.

The messages following weren't much use. They were mostly from other people expressing their shock and surprise.

After some thought, I typed a message and pressed send. "I was the one who found Martin this morning. Who is Jazz?"

It didn't take long for someone to reply.

Jazz Thompson, folk musician.

CHAPTER 10

I searched the internet for information about Jazz Thompson. Apparently, she was an up-and-coming folk artist in her twenties. Most of the information came from her social media accounts, and many of her posts were about future gigs. It seemed she was a full-time musician, which was something. I supposed it was no great surprise that Martin, the head of one of the biggest folk festivals in the country, had been seen talking to a folk musician. But what had happened after they left the pub? Did Martin meet someone else, or was Jazz the last person to see Martin?

The next day, I opened the tearoom on time. It quickly filled up, and I began to wish that Alan had started work today, rather than tomorrow. Even with Emma and Carole's help, things were pushed. Not that I was complaining. The popularity of the tearoom was beyond anything I'd ever hoped for.

Earlier, I had checked the messaging group to see if there had been any more comments about Martin. One message stood out. On the main committee's group chat, Laura had announced that Martin had died and she would be taking over as festival director, effective immediately.

That wasn't a surprise in itself, since I'd heard on the grapevine, that was what Martin had been training Laura for. The idea had been that she would take over the directorship the following year.

What did surprise me was that this year's festival hadn't been cancelled. Surely the death of the man who had been running it for so many years meant something? Then again, presumably because so many tickets had already been sold and the preparation done, it could be a financial disaster to cancel the festival at this late stage.

Later in the afternoon, during a welcome lull, I wandered to the front window. Laura was standing outside on the esplanade, talking to Danny Vance, the other member of Velvet Vortex who'd crashed the committee meeting.

My interest was piqued. Before I knew what I was doing, I found myself outside the tearoom and walking towards them. As soon as they saw me, they stopped talking.

Out of the corner of my eye, I could see all five ghosts. They couldn't go too far from the magical ring on my finger.

"Hello, Laura," I said. "How are things going?" I asked.

"Oh, Trinity, I'm rushed off my feet." She smoothed her hair, although it was not out of place. "You wouldn't believe how much work there is to do now that Martin has passed, uh, I mean, what a terrible thing to happen. And the police are saying it's murder." Her eyes narrowed slightly. "Have you heard anything, Trinity? Was it really you who found him?"

"Yes, it was, and it was definitely murder. I heard that straight from DI O'Malley."

"Do they know how he died?" She gave Danny a quick, sidelong glance.

I turned to Danny. "Did you see Martin the night he died?"

I saw Mr Wickers float towards Danny, waiting for his answer. His eyes were narrowed, and he had a quizzical expression. "Yes, good question. No point in beating around the bush, Trinity."

I wasn't sure why I'd asked that: it wasn't my place at all. But if anyone had had a motive to kill Martin, it was Danny surely? Maybe he'd met up with Martin the night he died. You could have cut the tension between them in that meeting with a knife.

"Who, me?" Danny took a step back. "Noooo. I was in my caravan with my girlfriend all night." He gave me a beady look. "Not that it's any of your business."

Mr Darby sniffed. "Murder is everyone's business."

I had to agree with Danny; it wasn't any of my business. "Oh, I'm sorry," I said. "I didn't mean to upset you, or to accuse you at all. I just wondered if you'd seen him. It's just that the police are trying to work out what happened and who Martin was with that evening."

Danny exhaled, and his aggression vanished. I chastised myself for being so obviously nosey. "I've already spoken to the police, actually. They came to see me yesterday. And I heard he was with Jazz Thompson that night."

I nodded, not indicating that this wasn't news to me.

Mr Wickers was still watching Danny closely. "DI Handsome, on the case. Admirable. Admirable."

"Look, I've got to go," Laura said suddenly. "I've got a million and one things to do."

"Oh, sorry, you must have," I said. "If there's anything I can do to help, just ask." I felt bad for not realising what a burden Laura now had to carry. There were only a few days until the folk festival started, and now Laura had to do it all without Martin.

Laura grabbed my arm. "Thank you, darling, that's so sweet of you. Must dash."

Danny nodded to me, then walked off along the esplanade with Laura. They didn't seem to be in much of a rush.

When I went back inside the tearoom, Lady Camilla

floated up to me. "You need to visit your friend Holly and find out if she knows anything more about the night Martin died."

Lady Camilla was right. But I hadn't heard from Holly since she'd popped in the previous morning, which meant she was probably extra busy. With a crafts and hobbies shop to run and a young family, she was always juggling several plates.

Despite that, as soon as I'd closed for the day, I ignored the tasks I had left, locked up, and walked the short distance to Holly's Craft Emporium.

Holly's shop was my oasis. I made any excuse to go there. I wasn't much of a crafts person, having failed dismally at knitting, crocheting, felting, embroidery, quilting, scrapbooking, painting, drawing, sewing, and paper crafting, among other things. But something about Holly's shop just made me happy.

Holly had recently changed her display window, and I stood looking at the fantastic creation she had put together. She'd outdone herself again. At the centre, a large table was covered with a patchwork quilt, displaying an array of hand-made treasures: mugs painted with intricate floral and folk designs, a knitted teddy bear wearing a traditional folk outfit, and colourful candles in mason jars decorated with rustic wool.

On the other side, small easels held watercolour paintings of the folk festival, capturing the dancing, music, and vibrant costumes. Paper flower garlands and bunting were draped across the display, and interspersed were dolls wearing traditional morris dance costumes, as well as straw hats adorned with ribbons, and small woven baskets filled with dried flowers and herbs.

"An admirable display." Mr Collingwood ventured.

I did a double take. "Yes it is, isn't it?"

A hand-lettered chalkboard read *Join Us for a Folk Festival*

Crafting Workshop! Another said, *New Arrivals: Folk Art and Festival Crafts!*

I smiled. Holly was always so talented when it came to art and crafts.

I went in and found her behind the counter, her laptop open.

Holly saw me and smiled. "What do you know?"

I grinned back. "You mean, what have I found out about the murder?"

"Yes, of course!"

"Well, not much more than I knew when you were in the tearoom yesterday. Oh, but I spoke to Danny Vance and Laura today. Danny denied having any involvement in Martin's murder. But the word is that the night Martin died, he had a late drink with a young folk artist called Jazz Thompson."

Holly scrunched up her nose. "I heard that, too."

"What else are people saying in the town?" I asked, knowing that Holly was always the centre of information.

"There are all sorts of wild conspiracy theories, as you'd expect. But Martin had made quite a lot of enemies lately, so it's not just Danny who's in the frame. Gordon Fisher is, too. He runs the crêpe stall at the festival, and he was seen arguing with Martin a few days ago. Apparently, he always has a pitch right outside the main entrance to the marquee. But this year, he's been put at the other end of the esplanade."

"I see." That was a bigger deal than it sounded. Gordon's new pitch was a long way from the main marquee, and that part of town was always a lot quieter, even during the folk festival.

"I take it Gordon was upset that he wasn't right in the centre of things."

"Yup. And interestingly, the ticket booth where Martin was found is right where Gordon's pitch used to be."

"Really?"

"Yep. It wasn't in previous years. The ticket booth used to be by the swimming pool."

"I'm sure that's just a coincidence."

Holly raised her eyebrows at me and said nothing.

I shook my head a little. "Well, anyway, it doesn't matter because I'm not investigating this murder. That's a job for the police. For DI O'Malley. And my cousin Francis."

Holly snorted. "Francis won't be any use. He's no detective."

"He's a good police officer, though."

Holly stayed silent. I glanced at the other side of the shop and saw the ghosts huddled around the beads. My eyebrows drew together. What were they up to? They weren't usually this quiet.

"You need to make a list of possible suspects," Holly said. "You cracked Clive's murder, and I'm sure you can crack this one." She stood up, picked up a plastic bag full of balls of pink wool, came out from behind the counter, and started placing the balls on a shelf.

"I can't. I'll be far too busy working. I'm expecting a bumper week, what with the festival."

"Everyone thinks it should be cancelled, out of respect."

"I thought so, too, at first, but there must be huge costs to cancelling. I mean, the festival is huge. Thousands of people come."

Holly sighed. "You're right. I hope someone will organise a memorial for Martin during the festival. It's the right thing to do."

"That's a lovely idea. I'll ask Laura. I'd better go now, though. We must catch up properly once the festival is over."

Holly nodded. "I'll pop into the tearoom when I can."

I glanced at the ghosts, who slunk away from the bead section, looking guilty. Hmmm. I walked over, wondering whether they'd discovered something.

I peered at the table and the wall display. All I could see

were beads in little packets. Then I gasped, and blushed. In the alphabet bead section, on the side, written out in beads, was "Trinity 4 OMalley".

Once we'd left Holly's shop, I glanced around to make sure no one was near, then spoke to the ghosts. "Since when have you been able to move objects in the real world?" I demanded.

The ghosts looked at each other, then at me, feigning innocence.

I sighed. "Come on, who did it? I know that Lily can move air, and Mr Collingwood can control electrics." I looked at Mr Darby. "Is your gift moving things?"

He raised his eyebrows.

Mr Wickers grinned at Mr Darby.

"What about you?" I shot at him.

His face fell. "Me? I don't have the gift of moving things."

I studied Lady Camilla. "I can't imagine you would write anything like that."

She nodded approvingly. "You are correct, young lady. I would never have written anything so common."

"One of you did it." I put my hand on my hip and looked from one to the other. "Well? Which of you can move objects?"

They all hung their heads, but none of them spoke.

"It was either Mr Wickers or Mr Darby. And from what was written, I surmise it was Mr Wickers."

A small smile played on his lips. I was right.

I opened my mouth to speak again, but a couple walked past, so I closed it again. I didn't want to appear mad.

I walked back to the tearoom to finish clearing up and prepare for the next day.

Mr Darby floated next to me as I wiped a table. "If you are investigating who the murderer is, you must speak to the prime suspect."

I stopped wiping and looked at him, cloth in hand. "Who?"

"Danny Vance, of course. Their past connection in a musical group and its subsequent break-up mean he must be the prime suspect."

"But Martin was last seen with Jazz Thompson. Surely she'd be my first port of call."

Mr Darby shook his head. "Too obvious. She's too young. Martin would have been much older than her. What would her motive be?"

"No idea. That's why I need to speak to her."

"You need to speak to both of them. Start with the most likely. That is Danny."

I sighed. "I've already asked him if he saw Martin the night he died. He denied it."

"He could be lying. Try again."

"All right. But first I need to find out where he's staying. He mentioned a caravan, but in a seaside resort like Sidmouth, it doesn't narrow it down much."

Mr Darby thought for a moment, hovering. "Try the messaging on your phone with the other café and restaurant owners," he said, at last.

I typed a quick message to everyone in the group. Within minutes, someone told me he was staying at the caravan park a few miles along the coast towards Budleigh Salterton.

CHAPTER 11

Why was Danny staying in a caravan park out of town, rather than an expensive hotel on the seafront? He'd told us in the committee meeting the day before that he'd been making connections with people in the music industry. Surely that would be very profitable?

I looked online and found very little about what Danny Vance had been doing since his glory days in Velvet Vortex. My mind raced with what might have happened in the intervening years.

I'd heard that despite wild success in groups and bands, most musicians who made it big didn't make much money. The record companies and the song writers cashed in, rather than the performers. Perhaps despite his youthful fame, money hadn't come to him.

Alternatively, if he had made money along with his fame, it was possible he'd spent it all. It was a long time ago.

I drove to see Danny and the ghosts came with me, as they were all eager to see the caravan park. They told me on the way, they had seen caravan parks before, though not this specific one. I still wanted to know all about the past ring-owners, but the ghosts remained tight-lipped about it.

When we reached the caravan park, there were at least fifty caravans. How to find out which one was Danny's hadn't even occurred to me. A small brick building had a sign which said Reception and Shop, but it was closed. "There's only one thing to do," I said. "I'll have to start knocking on caravan doors."

"There's no need for that," said Mr Darby. "We'll find him for you." He turned to the other ghosts. "Spread out and start checking every caravan for Danny Vance."

I was relieved. It could have taken me ages to knock on every door to find Danny. I hung around by the reception building, trying not to look too suspicious.

A couple of minutes after the ghosts had dispersed, I heard a shriek.

"Well, I never!" cried Lady Camilla. "What shocking behaviour." She passed through the wall of a nearby caravan and floated above it, looking disgusted.

"What is it?" I asked.

"I will not speak of it," she said, with disdain.

Perhaps it was better not to know. "Nothing illegal, I hope," I said, as she disappeared into the next van.

"Over here!" called Mr Wickers, a few minutes later. "Caravan twenty-four."

I weaved between the vans, keeping an eye out for the numbers painted near the doors and found number twenty-four.

The outside of the caravan was pristine, the kind you'd expect to find in a glossy brochure for a high-end park like this. It had a sleek, modern design with clean white panels. A small wooden deck extended from the front, complete with neatly arranged outdoor furniture and a potted plant by the steps, giving it the feel of a cozy holiday retreat.

The ghosts gathered behind me, except for Mr Wickers, whose head suddenly poked through the side of the caravan.

I gasped and clutched my chest. "Stop doing that! You know how I feel about you you appearing through walls."

"My apologies, madam." Mr Wickers gave me a small nod, his expression contrite, but there was a definite twinkle in his eye.

I knocked, and to my surprise, a woman opened the caravan door. She was at least fifty, with peroxide-blonde hair, wearing multicoloured leggings and a vest top, which clung to her petite figure. She looked me up and down with a sneer. "Yeah?"

"Hi, I'm looking for Danny Vance. Is he in?"

"You and all the other women." She sighed theatrically and rolled her eyes. "Look, love, you can see Danny at the festival. He'll sign a photo. You shouldn't be coming round here trying to get to see him. That's stalking, you know."

I gaped at her. "Stalking? Oh no, I just need to talk to Danny about what happened the other night." I paused for a moment realising what I'd said could be misconstrued. "I mean, not anything like *that*. I'm Trinity, one of the folk festival committee members."

"What?" She paused for a moment, processing what I'd told her. "Wait there." She disappeared inside.

"She could have asked you in," Lady Camilla said, wrinkling her nose. "And not only that, she is dressed most peculiarly."

Mr Collingwood nodded and bowed. "Indeed, she is. While I commend her courage in embracing such an unusual choice of attire, it does strike me as rather unbecoming for a lady. One must always strive for propriety, after all."

A moment later, Danny appeared. "Oh, it's you," he said. "What's the problem?"

"No problem, I-I just wanted to ask about the other night."

"We've already talked about it. I told you where I was." He indicated to the inside of the caravan. "I was here, with my girlfriend, Denise."

"I wanted to ask you what you remember about meeting up with Martin. Can I come in?"

He hesitated for a moment. "I suppose. It's a bit of a mess, though."

"It is," said Mr. Wickers, from inside the caravan. "You must prepare yourself, madam."

I stepped in. The caravan was bigger than I thought and modern. Not luxurious, but very comfortable. However, empty beer cans, crisp packets, shoes, and clothes were strewn over the floor. In the small kitchen area, unwashed pans and crockery sat in the sink.

"Take a seat," he said, moving a bag from the settee. I had just about enough room to sit down.

"Thanks," I said perching myself on the small space.

"So, are you one of those nosey women who try and solve murders?" He laughed a sharp, barking sound that echoed in the small room.

I didn't much like Danny's description, but I decided it might be useful. "Well, yes, I suppose I am. So I want to find out everything I can about Martin's movements that night. It seems he hung around town rather than going home. Did you see him?"

"Like I told you yesterday, I came back here nice and early with Denise."

Denise had disappeared as soon as I came in. I assumed she'd gone into the bedroom.

"So you didn't see him at all?" I asked.

He stared at me. Eventually, he spoke. "No."

"He's lying." Mr Wickers was next to Danny, staring at his face.

Mr Darby smirked. "Takes one to know one."

"Stop arguing, you two," Lady Camilla scolded.

I nodded, not knowing what else to say. I'd expected Danny to say that he had seen Martin. That, perhaps, after their run-in at the meeting, they'd had a massive argument.

That made sense to me. Then they would either have gone their separate ways, or Danny would have. I made a mental note to plan what to ask next time I went investigating.

"So, um, why did your band break up?"

Danny shrugged. "Artistic differences."

I frowned. "What does that mean?"

"It means that we both wrote songs, but only his got recorded and released. He was the lead singer, but I was just as good as him. So I got fed up with playing second fiddle."

"You both played guitar?"

Danny shrugged. "Martin made me play bass. Said one guitarist was enough."

I remembered Velvet Vortex breaking up. I'd been a young child in their heyday, but they got progressively less famous the older I grew. Although I hadn't been much of a fan, I recalled hearing about their breakup in one of the teen magazines I'd read at the time. I made a mental note to look it up on the internet when I got home. *Home.* Yes, and I needed to feed Wentworth, my Russian blue cat. He'd be waiting for me.

"So when was the last time you spoke to Martin? You must have seen him since the committee meeting?"

"We saw each other around town now and again over the next few days. He wouldn't speak to me. Do you know he fired Sarah, the festival coordinator? All because she got me to come and improve the festival."

"Really?" That was news to me.

"Yeah, and with less than a week to go till the festival start. I mean, Martin didn't like me, fair enough, but to fire someone because of me. That's low. Don't you think?" Danny sniffed.

I made a mental note to add Sarah to the suspect list.

"So, did you go solo after the band broke up?" I asked.

Danny's face darkened. "Yeah. Didn't score any hits, though. That was because the record company put all their money into Martin. After my second release didn't make the charts, they dumped me. Their loss though."

"Oh dear, that's a shame. It must have made you resent Martin."

His eyes narrowed. "Are you fishing for a motive? I hope you're not trying to stitch me up."

I had been looking for a motive, of course, and foolishly thinking aloud. I needed to be more careful. "Oh no, of course not. Sorry. I was just thinking of how I would feel in your situation. You know, if that had happened to me."

That seemed to mollify him. I decided to leave before I put my foot in my mouth again. "Thank you for seeing me, Danny. I'd better get going. Always things to do in the tearoom."

"At this time?" He studied me, with an odd expression on his face. "Well, I'm sure I'll see you around the festival."

"Um, you're very welcome to come into the tearoom for a complimentary cream tea," I gabbled.

His expression didn't change. "Thanks very much. No offense, but a Jane Austen tearoom is not really my scene. I'll bear that in mind, though. Denise might want to go."

CHAPTER 12

As soon as I got home, Wentworth, my rescued and adopted Russian blue cat, was winding around my legs, meowing. I picked him up and cuddled him, wondering how anyone could have dumped him in a field. Not only was he cute and friendly, but he could see the ghosts.

Eventually Wentworth wriggled out of my grasp, and I put food down for him.

We all watched him eat. "What did you think of Danny?" I asked the ghosts.

"Slippery man," Mr. Wickers stated, still looking at Wentworth.

"Do you still think he was telling the truth about not seeing Martin after the meeting?"

"I think he was lying. Maybe you should do some further investigation into his movements the night before."

"I can't see how. It's not like we can track his mobile phone data."

There was a long silence as we all contemplated what to do next.

Mr. Collingwood cleared his throat. "In the meantime,

madam, may I request that we investigate the magical moonstone?"

Oh yes, the magical moonstone. Not long after the tearoom had opened, Mr. Collingwood had requested that I help him and the other ghosts to reach the afterlife. Somehow, the ghosts had all become attached to the turquoise ring formerly owned by Jane Austen, and which now sat on my finger. The ghosts thought it was some kind of deep magic.

All the ghosts had died in the same fire, which had taken place just outside Winchester in 1797. They had gone to bed at the inn as people, and awakened as ghosts attached to the ring. However, something was keeping them from passing into the afterlife. Understandably, after hundreds of years as ghosts, they wanted to move on.

Mr. Collingwood had told me about a treasure map made by a well-known nineteenth-century Sidmouth pirate called Black-Eye Elmore, which would lead to a hidden treasure that would help them get to the afterlife. How, I had no idea, and I was sure Mr Collingwood didn't either. After searching two different pubs in Sidmouth, the ghosts had found the map. However, the map was guarded by another ghost, Betsy Knight, who could only release the map when given an enchanted moonstone by a direct descendent of Black-Eye Elmore.

I hadn't even begun searching for descendants of Black-Eye Elmore, though. That was pointless until we had the enchanted moonstone. I wasn't even sure if there was a specific enchanted moonstone we needed to find, or whether any enchanted moonstone would do. Betsy Knight hadn't been helpful at all, because she'd been turned into a ghost especially to guard the map.

I sighed. "All right. First thing tomorrow, I'll go to the crystal shop and see if the owner knows anything about enchanted moonstones."

Mr. Collingwood, an ever-polite man, bowed in gratitude.

The next day, true to my word, I visited the crystal shop.

Mystic Sparkle was a small shop on the high street, nestled between a boutique and a candle shop. It had a bright turquoise exterior, and inside, the crisp white walls were filled with case after case of exquisite crystal jewellery. In the middle was a table displaying individual stones and crystals.

It was early, and I was the only customer. As soon as I entered, I felt warm and happy. I'd noticed it before in other crystal shops: a sort of strange radiance coming from the stones. I couldn't put my finger on what it was, but being around crystals made me peaceful.

Behind a desk on the far right was a woman in her late fifties, tall, with long blonde hair in a ponytail, and glasses. She said hello as I walked in, then carried on sorting earrings.

I started to browse the glass cabinets, and the ghosts spread out, searching, too.

Mr Wickers stood right in the middle of the table of crystals and stones, a dreamy look on his face. "Oh yes! The energy from these stones is wonderful. It makes me feel elated."

Lady Camilla tutted at him and floated into the stockroom at the back, Mr Collingwood in her wake.

"Your moonstone jewellery is lovely," I said to the woman at the desk.

She smiled. "Thanks. I like their milkiness."

I moved a little closer. "Have you ever heard of an enchanted moonstone?"

She took off her glasses. "No, I can't say that I have. Enchanted amber, yes, but not moonstone."

"What do you know about enchanted amber?" I asked, hoping there might be a connection.

"Well, some say it has healing powers, and also the power to influence people."

"Have you heard of any other stones or crystals with powers?"

"All the stones and crystals are good for something. But moonstones? No, not beyond the usual claims. Lots of cultures revere moonstones, though. Talking about an enchanted moonstone might be a way to secure a higher price for it by trading on people's wishful thinking. Why do you ask?"

If I told her the whole truth, she would think I was nuts. But maybe there was another way. "I'm on a quest to find an enchanted moonstone," I said. "Seriously, if I told you the reason why, you wouldn't believe me. But it's fascinating."

Her mouth curled up on one side. "That sounds very mysterious and intriguing. I'm sorry I can't help you any further."

I continued to browse a different cabinet. "Oh, one other thing. Do you know anything about Black-Eye Elmore, the famous Sidmouth pirate?"

She looked confused. "I've heard of him, but I don't know much more than what you've said. There'll be plenty about him in the museum."

The museum! I hadn't visited it since I was a child. "Thanks! I'll pay it a visit."

CHAPTER 13

"Ooh, the museum." Lily bobbed up and down excitedly as we approached the white building next to the parish church in the middle of the town.

I tried to remember my impressions of it as a child, but it was so long ago that I couldn't recall. Anyway, things were bound to have changed inside by now.

The museum was an old, white rendered building in the heart of the town. I stepped inside and paid the small entry fee to the elderly man behind the desk. He wore a badge saying "Volunteer".

"Can you tell me where your information on Black-Eye Elmore is located?"

"First floor. Through there, up the stairs."

I made my way straight up. It was quiet. I couldn't see any other visitors. The stairs led to a huge room filled with displays about Black-Eye Elmore.

To my left was a display with a mannequin, and underneath a plaque: "Black-Eye Elmore." The mannequin was dressed like a pirate. He had a crimson waistcoat with tarnished brass buttons, a billowing white shirt with cuffs that spilled out, and a pair of dark, weathered brown breeches. A wide leather belt with an oversized buckle slung across its hips, and a faded sash of gold and green.

On its head sat a tricorn hat, slightly askew, with a black feather drooping over one side. Around its neck hung a string of cheap imitation pearls, and an eyepatch covered one eye, completing the look. Not quite Jack Sparrow, but close enough.

I walked closer, and that must have set off a movement sensor, as I heard waves breaking and seagull cries, then a man talking in a west country accent. "Who be you?" he said. "I be Black-Eye Elmore, fearsome pirate. I roam the English Channel, running from ye Royal Navy, but they never get me. Arrrrr!"

I cringed. I hadn't expected Madam Tussaud's, but the crackling audio and cheesy accent was embarrassingly bad.

Black-Eye appeared to be standing in a dimly lit tavern, his pose frozen, one hand resting on the hilt of a cutlass while the other held a pewter tankard. Around him, kegs and barrels were stacked haphazardly, their wooden surfaces aged and splintered, with faded markings hinting at their contents: ale, or something stronger, rum. A nearby wooden table was cluttered with objects meant to complete the seventeenth-century scene: brass candlesticks dripping with artificial wax, a pair of snuffers, and a long-stemmed pipe.

Hanging from a beam above was an old wooden inn sign with weathered letters, reading The Ship Inn. I'd been in that building many times. One time an inn, but now a coffee shop.

The scene's backdrop had been painted to resemble rough wooden walls, with faint streaks of grime added for authenticity. "I'm sure he wasn't that handsome," Lady Camilla observed, nose in the air. "I never met him, of course, but a pirate would be much more weather-beaten. And battle-scarred."

I continued walking around the displays. There was a

map of the coast, showing Sidmouth and other coastal towns where Black-Eye Elmore's crew were supposed to have lived. There was also a picture of his ship, the *Crimson Tide*.

Then I came to a glass-topped case with items displayed inside. As I looked down, a wave of something like electricity flowed through me, and my hand was pulled to the case.

"W-what the…"

The ghosts sped over: they sensed it, too.

Lady Camilla put her head through the glass. "It's that ring."

"We can't see," complained Mr Darby. "Not with your head and her hand in the way."

"It's a gold ring set with an oval moonstone," Lady Camilla reported.

I moved my hand away, with difficulty – the turquoise ring I wore felt as if it had been magnetised – and read the inscription below the ring. "'*A gold moonstone ring believed to have belonged to Black-Eye Elmore.*' How would they know it was his?"

Mr. Darby put a finger on his chin. "That is a very good question, madam, but as your ring and that ring are attracted to each other, there's a very good chance that this is the enchanted moonstone required in exchange for the map."

Lady Camilla lifted her head out of the case and looked at him. "I think you're right. I can feel it emanating magic."

I tried to move my hand away from the case, but it was too difficult. I could only get away by taking a long step back. Then the magnetic feeling stopped.

Mr Collingwood floated over to me, an urgent expression on his face. "You have to take that ring," he said.

Mr Wickers smirked. "You, a man of the cloth, advocating theft."

Mr Collingwood scowled. "If that is the enchanted moonstone ring, then it does not belong to this museum. It belongs to us."

"He has a point," I said.

"The case is locked," said Mr Collingwood, pointing to the keyhole in the wooden frame. "You will have to break it open."

I stared at him. "I'm not doing that. Besides, look over there." I indicated a CCTV camera on a bracket near the ceiling.

"You could volunteer as a helper," Mr Collingwood suggested. "Then, when they leave you here to look after the museum, you could switch off the camera and take the ring."

"Then they'd definitely know it was me, because the ring would have gone missing when I was volunteering. And anyway, I can't volunteer here. I don't have time. I have the tearoom to run, I'm on the folk festival committee, and I have you ghosts to look after." The thought of taking on even more responsibilities made me panic. Not to mention the thought of committing a crime.

"I object to your last remark, madam," said Mr Darby. "*We* do not need looking after."

"Yes you do. I'm your portal to the outside world. Plus, I'm trying to get you all to the afterlife, in case you've forgotten that minor detail."

Mr Darby's eyes narrowed. For a moment I felt like Elizabeth Bennet, being scrutinised by Mr Darcy when they were sparring at Netherfield. He said no more but floated through the wall, probably as far away from me as possible.

"*We* can't steal it," Lily said. "We can't lift things like this."

"Can't you whip up a small whirlwind?"

"Not that small, no."

I looked over to Mr Wickers. "You can move beads; surely you can move a small ring?"

"I can't open locks," he replied.

"*I* can't steal it," I hissed.

"Then, madam, how do you propose to get the map without it?" Mr Collingwood asked.

He had a point. But I couldn't believe I was actually contemplating stealing something from a museum.

"All this talk of stealing is silly," Lady Camilla stated. "All the museum wants is a moonstone ring in that case. They're not going to do anything with that ring, whereas our plans – our *lives* – depend upon it. What you must do is take a photograph of the ring, commission someone to make a replica, and swap it for the real ring. Then no one but us will be any the wiser."

I stared at her. "Is that what happened with this?" I looked at the turquoise ring on my finger. Jane Austen's actual turquoise ring, that she had worn.

"It is. The one in the Jane Austen House Museum is a fake."

I let out a sigh. I despised stealing, but this was a special case. I'd promised to help the ghosts get to the afterlife, and the map was the only way. "All right, I'll do it."

I took out my phone, momentarily took the turquoise ring off freeing my hands from the pull between the rings, and then shot photos of the moonstone ring from every angle, then left the museum.

Later, I messaged Holly, who gave me the number of a local friend who made bespoke jewellery. After a short phone call, followed by an email, she agreed to make a replica of the ring, but she wouldn't be able to start it for at least a week. I didn't mind, though. That gave me some time to work out how I could possibly swap the rings.

CHAPTER 14

The following morning, I decided to go for another early walk along the esplanade. I couldn't help remembering what I'd come across the last time I'd walked out. I tried to focus on the town coming to life through the festival, rather than Martin's lifeless body.

What were the chances of stumbling into another dead body? Slim, but not zero. But at least I had the ghosts to keep me from melancholy.

They floated next to me as I walked, commenting occasionally.

The cool breeze from the seafront was refreshing, and the soft smell of salt and seaweed reminded me of my childhood walks in the very same place. I was still glad to be back home, and I realised I'd hardly thought of London lately.

The sky was a canvas of pastel colours, the first rays of sunlight just beginning to peek over the horizon.

At the far end of the esplanade a row of food vendor tents stretched out before me, a colourful array of structures whose bunting and banners flapped gently in the morning breeze.

Then I caught sight of one of the signs: Holy Crêpe. I remembered what Holly had told me about the owner,

Gordon Fisher. He'd been angry with Martin and argued with him, because Martin had moved him from his usual prime pitch outside the marquee to the far end of the esplanade, well away from the festival hub.

The crêpe tent was already open for business. There was a big open sign on the side, and a customer was stood a short distance away with a crêpe in his hands. Being open at this time surprised me. How many people would want a crêpe at this time of day? A least one person, it seemed.

The menu at the side of the tent had a list of breakfast crêpes, Mr Wickers and Lily both examined the menu with me:

Classic Ham & Cheese Crêpe: Thin slices of ham and melted cheese folded into a warm crêpe.
Bacon & Egg Crêpe: Crispy bacon and a fried egg topped with a sprinkle of chives.
Smoked Salmon & Cream Cheese Crêpe: Delicate smoked salmon with a layer of cream cheese and a hint of dill.

"Interesting breakfast menu," Mr Wickers commented.

I nodded. I was hungry, but I had plenty of food in the tearoom.

Inside the tent, Gordon Fisher stood, his back to me.

"Hello," I called out, stepping closer.

Gordon turned and smiled at me. "What can I get you, love?"

He was a tall, stocky man in his sixties, with long grey hair tied back in a ponytail. He smiled, revealing tobacco-stained teeth.

"Oh, er, nothing at the moment. I wanted to introduce myself. I'm Trinity Bishop, the folk festival committee liaison for restaurants and cafés. I own the Regency Tearoom on the front."

Recognition sparked in his eyes. "Ah, yes, the historical tearoom. I'm Gordon." He smiled and nodded, though not offering his hand to shake.

"I was also the person who found Martin's body." I glanced towards the back of the tent, where boxes of supplies were neatly stacked.

Gordon's expression darkened. "Nasty business, that. I can't imagine what you must have gone through, finding him like that," he said, his voice tinged with what sounded like genuine sympathy.

"How long had you known Martin?" I asked, deflecting.

Mr Darby floated through the tent, next to Gordon, and started inspecting him and the inside of the tent.

Gordon raised his eyebrows and put his hands in his pockets. "Since he took over running the festival."

"Did you know him well? I only met him once."

"Well enough. Talked occasionally each year here at the festival. Sad he's gone. I don't like to speak ill of dead ... but..." He stopped but my interest was peaked. He clearly wanted to say something about Martin, and I wanted to hear it.

"It's not speaking ill of the dead if you speak facts," I prompted, hoping he'd open up. It worked.

"He shafted me, good and proper. I used to have my pitch by the main entrance of the main festival area, you know. Best spot in the place."

I did know.

Gordon continued. "Then a few months ago, he told me I'd have to bung him five hundred quid in cash to keep my usual pitch. He said that if I didn't, he'd give it to someone else. I didn't believe he'd do it, so I told him what I thought of him and said he could take a running jump." He huffed. "And that was that. Here I am."

The current tent pitch was a lot farther out, away from the main festival areas. It was isolated compared to the location near the main marquee. This spot, while not terrible, would miss most of the foot traffic. A pang of sympathy hit me as I imagined Gordon's disappointment and frustration at being ousted from his usual spot.

"Did you complain to the committee, or Laura or Sarah?" I asked, curious as to how these sorts of disputes were typically resolved.

"Yeah, but they didn't believe me," Gordon said, with a wry smile. "Martin fed them some cock-and-bull story that I'd made up the whole thing and they believed him. Always knew how to talk his way out of trouble, that one."

I pondered his words. If what Gordon said was true, it painted a picture of Martin as a man who would not hesitate to use his position for personal gain. But surely anger and frustration alone wouldn't drive someone to murder. Or could it? Could Gordon have had something to do with Martin's murder?

Mr. Darby floated over a jar on the counter, peering at the label. "Peanut butter? On a crêpe?" His nose wrinkled in disgust.

"Did you see Martin the night he was murdered?" I asked, watching Gordon's face closely and ignoring Mr Darby.

Gordon nodded slowly. "Yeah, I saw him but I didn't speak to him. He was walking along the esplanade with that folk musician. What's her name now?" He scratched his head. "Jazz something, that's it."

"Was anyone else with him?"

He hesitated for a moment. "No, it was just the two of them."

"What time was that?" I asked, mentally piecing together a timeline of Martin's last known movements.

"About seven. I remember, because the church bells had just finished ringing, and I was packing up for the day."

"Is she famous in the folk world?" I asked, wondering what connection, if any, existed between the two.

Gordon shrugged. "Not really. She's playing a couple of gigs at the festival, but she's only been going a short while." Gordon's tone had shifted to one of admiration. "She's got talent, though. Heard her sing yesterday. Busking, she was. She'll go far, if she gets the right breaks."

"I'll check the festival programme and see if I can make one of her gigs," I said.

"Are you sure I can't get you anything?" Gordon pointed to the menu on the side.

"Go on, I'll have a ham and cheese."

"Great choice." He picked up the batter jug, whistling.

CHAPTER 15

fter my walk, I got to the tearoom a little earlier than usual because it would be Alan's first day. Alan appeared at the front door at a quarter to ten sharp. I opened the door and looked him up and down. "Well, don't you look dashing."

Alan was dressed in full Regency costume: black riding boots, tan breeches, white shirt, cream waistcoat and cravat, and a dark green tailcoat. He looked perfect. A wave of happiness from having him around washed over me.

The ghosts all gathered around to inspect Alan's costume, too.

Lily whizzed around him. "He looks very handsome."

Lady Camilla agreed, "Yes indeed. I approve."

I looked over to Mr Darby; I caught his eye. "Very smart."

I clapped my hands, thankful that the ghosts approved. "So who will you be today? Mr Bennet?" I asked Alan.

"Mr. Bennet to start with, don't you think?"

"Excellent. Now let me show you the ropes, although today I'll just ask you to greet the customers, chat to them at the tables, and clear away. Nothing too strenuous." Now that

I'd seen his costume, I wondered if I could persuade him to stand outside, too, as a sort of live advertisement.

"I could spend some time outside the tearoom, too," Alan said. "You know, persuading people to come inside."

I blinked. "Um, yes. That's a great idea. You can do that, but later on. Maybe if it gets quiet."

He nodded and followed me into the kitchen.

As the morning progressed, Alan fully embraced his role as Mr. Bennet. He stood at the entrance, greeting each customer with a warm smile and a gracious bow.

A group of women entered, their faces lighting up as they took in Alan's Regency attire. "Ladies, welcome to our humble establishment," he said, in the affable tones of Mr. Bennet. "May I introduce myself? My name is Mr Bennet. I trust you are ready to partake of some refreshments and enjoy some lively conversation?"

The women giggled, clearly delighted by his performance. "Indeed, Mr. Bennet," one replied. "We have heard much about your hospitality."

Alan led them to a table near the window. "I can recommend the Earl Grey tea: it does wonders for Mrs Bennet's nerves. And as you know, her nerves are no trifling matter!"

They giggled again.

It wasn't until the afternoon that I remembered I needed to talk to Jazz Thompson, the performer whom several witnesses had seen with Martin on the night he was murdered. In a brief lull, I went into the kitchen and checked my phone to see if she had posted about any new local gigs on her social media feeds.

I was in luck. There was a new post on her Instagram feed, with a photo of the esplanade. *Catch me here every afternoon, when I try out some new material for my upcoming festival gigs.*

I went to the front door and looked out. She was there. I listened. Sure enough, I could hear an acoustic guitar and a woman's voice singing a plaintive melody.

Alan had been nearby and glanced at me. "Not exactly the sort of music the Bennet sisters would have played, is it?"

"Not quite, no." I glanced around the tearoom. The afternoon rush was over now. Carole and Emma could easily manage if I nipped outside for a few minutes. "Back in a mo." And off I went.

Jazz Thompson was standing on the opposite side of the esplanade, strumming a guitar plugged into an amplifier and singing a song I didn't recognise. A few people were standing around, listening. She looked similar to her social media profile, but she was more petite than I'd thought. She had curly brown hair in a messy bun, a silver nose hoop and mismatched earrings climbing her ear. That matched her boho-style dungarees and with thick boots. I couldn't help thinking her feet would get hot in those in the summer.

When the song ended, I moved forward and put a few coins into the open guitar case in front of her. There seemed to be quite a lot of money in it already, including a couple of notes.

"Thank you," she said, giving my Regency dress a quizzical look.

"Was that your own song? It was lovely."

"Yes, it was. Thank you. It's very kind of you to say."

"Are you playing at the festival?" Even though I knew she was, I needed to keep the conversation going.

"I have a couple of gigs. Nothing too big." She leaned down to pick up a bottle of water and took a swig from it. Lady Camilla inspected her, disapprovement all over her face. I gave her an inquisitive look.

"Singing in public places is vulgar," she commented, answering my question.

"How did you get into the festival line-up?"

She smiled. "Oh, you know, the usual way. I know a few people in the industry, and Martin Hawthorne is – well, was –

one of them. I don't know if you know, but he died just a couple of days ago."

"Yes. That was very unfortunate, wasn't it? Poor man." I didn't mention I was the one who'd found him dead.

"He was mentoring me. He said I could go far in the folk world." She looked misty-eyed. "That's all I've ever dreamed of since I was young."

You're still young, I thought, but I suppose she meant from when she was a child.

"When did you last see Martin?" I asked, trying to keep my voice casual.

Jazz sighed. "That's the thing: I saw him on the night he died. He'd been so busy that day, but he still found time for a drink and a chat with me. He spent a lot of time helping me."

"Don't you think that's a bit strange? A man of his age, taking all that time to help a young girl like you?" In fact, it wasn't strange; it was a tale as old as time, but I wanted to point it out.

My question changed the tone of our conversation instantly. She frowned. "What do you mean?"

"Well, you don't look any older than twenty, and Martin was at least sixty."

Jazz took a step back, her face stony. "If you're implying what it sounds like, it wasn't like that at all. He just wanted to help, that's all."

I suspected a lot of older men were keen to help others, as long as they were young, female, and pretty, but I didn't want to get into an argument. I wanted more information. "I'm sure he did," I said, "and that was kind of him. Sorry, I didn't mean to be so blunt. I'm glad he helped you. How did you get to know Martin in the first place?"

Jazz looked slightly defensive. "My mum spoke to Martin at the festival a couple of years ago. She played him a couple of video clips of me singing and asked if he'd help me get a foot in the door. I couldn't believe it when he said yes."

I could. "So he was giving you advice?"

"Yeah. And he had industry contacts, too. Not that that's any use, now that he's dead."

"And is your mum here, at the festival?"

"Not this year." She shifted from foot to foot. "Look, it's been nice to chat, but I need to get back to playing. Now I've not got Martin's help any more, I need to make my own opportunities."

I looked around me: the small crowd of spectators had drifted away. "Sure. I'm sorry for interrupting." I turned to go back to the tearoom.

Mr Wickers winked at me. "I don't believe Martin's motivation was pure regarding that young lady."

"You would say that," replied Mr Darby. "If I befriended a young lady, it would be for pure reasons."

"I'm sure it would be," I said, honestly.

Mr Wickers shook his head at Mr Darby. "Always the consummate gentleman. Booooringgg."

I huffed. "The thing is, we know Jazz met up with Martin on the night he was murdered, but she had no reason to kill him. She wouldn't have wanted to because she'd lose out on Martin's help and influence if he died. Which he did."

"True," Mr Wickers said. He sighed. "So I suppose she's off the hook."

I nodded. "Yes, I suppose she is."

CHAPTER 16

The following day, Laura sent me a message that she would pop into the tearoom that afternoon to check a few things with me. I was pleased. I could take the opportunity to ask her about Martin.

She came in at three, flustered and harassed-looking. But Alan worked his charm on her, and her mood lifted. He seated her at a table near the kitchen and I joined her, bringing a pot of tea and some Devon apple cake with me. "I expect you haven't stopped all day," I said, looking at her across the table.

Laura pulled an A4 folder from her bag, flicked through the contents, and let out an exasperated sigh. "You wouldn't believe how frantic things have been. Without Martin, I've got double the load."

"Oh dear. Can't anyone help you?"

"No one knows enough of the details to help."

I frowned. "Not even Sarah? Isn't she the festival coordinator?"

"Sarah was fired by Martin – before he died, of course – for bringing Danny into the fold. They had an argument after the meeting that night. I've asked her to come back, but she's refusing."

"How do you know they had a argument?"

Laura shrugged. "I heard about it from both of them. They both told me about it the day after. Separately, of course."

"But he's not in charge any more. So why won't she continue?"

Laura shrugged. "She said she'd had more than enough of the festival. Her timing's shocking."

"Surely someone can help." I hoped she wasn't about to ask me to step up. I already had too much on my plate.

"Plenty of people have offered, but it's quicker to do stuff myself." She ate a forkful of the apple cake. "Mmm, this is divine."

"I know what you mean: by the time you've explained how to do something, you could have done it yourself." I poured the tea and handed a cup and saucer to Laura. "Is there much you need to tell me, then?"

"Not much. Just that we're expecting a bumper amount of people this time. The campsite has sold out, so it might be prudent for you to suggest people extend their opening hours. It's going to be extremely busy."

That would be good for my tearoom. I'd see how busy it got on the first day of the festival. If there were enough people looking for somewhere to have tea and scones, I could definitely stay open longer than usual.

"I'll let everybody know."

"There's not much else. Oh, except that we have a couple of sponsorship spaces for the best female morris group and best young male vocalist. We really need to fill those."

"Tell me about that." I wondered whether my marketing budget could stretch that far.

"The sponsorship spaces are one hundred pounds per award, and you get to present the award at the event. Your business will be in the festival programme as a sponsor."

That sounded quite reasonable. "Okay, I'll do the female

morris group. And I'll post on the messaging group about the other one."

Laura wrote on her notepad. Her squiggly handwriting was too tricky for my dyslexic brain to read upside down. Then she attacked the cake again, and I used the opportunity to pump her for more information.

"So, do you know much yet about what happened to Martin on the night he was killed?"

"Not much," Laura said between mouthfuls. "We'd spent most of that day sorting out all kinds of problems. Honestly, after all these years you'd think things would run smoothly, but they never do."

"How many years had you been working with Martin on the festival?"

"Five up till now. He was training me to take over from him eventually, although we'd never settled when that would happen. Every year, Martin said it would be his last one, and then he carried on. Mind you, now that he has gone, I'd like him back in a flash. I've had so many people telling me I should have cancelled the whole festival. But we can't: the event insurance doesn't cover the murder of our director. We never thought to put that in the insurance clauses." She let out a bitter laugh.

"Was he married?"

"No, never. He was a bit of a ladies' man."

I hadn't heard that term for a while. My son, Oliver, used the term 'player'. "Oh? Did he have a girlfriend or two?"

Laura snorted. "More than that. He always had a different woman on his arm, and sometimes more than one on the go at once. Some of them got a kick out of being seen with who he used to be – famous back in the day – and some just fell for his charms."

I thought back to the committee meeting. Martin hadn't struck me as a particularly charming man, but perhaps that was because he was under a lot of stress running the festival. That, and the fact that his former bandmate had suddenly turned up.

Laura ate another bite of apple cake. "You have to give me the recipe for this."

I nursed my cup of tea and thought. If Martin had been a ladies' man, maybe one of them had got jealous. My best friend, Holly, would be the best person to ask about that.

"So, when did you last see Martin on the day he died?"

"Me and Martin parted company before seven pm. He left to meet with that girl, the singer."

"Jazz Thompson?"

Laura's face darkened. "That's the one."

"She was busking on the esplanade yesterday and I thought she was good. She told me Martin was mentoring her. She seemed to be telling the truth."

Laura's mouth curved in a twisted smile. "I'm sure she is, just like all the others. He'd pick a pretty young thing every year and 'mentor' her. Till he met another one." It didn't take Sherlock Holmes to know what she meant. "Sounds like Jazz has had a lucky escape, then," I commented.

Laura finished the cake, then drained her teacup and stood up. "Must dash: still so much to do. Honestly, whoever killed Martin could have waited until after the festival. It's most inconvenient."

When she'd left, I stayed seated for a few minutes. The ghosts had been listening to our conversation.

"She needs better table manners," Lady Camilla stated as she sat exactly where Laura had a few moments before.

Mr Collingwood stood next to her and bowed. "Indeed, Your Ladyship."

Mr Darby came from across the room. "If that lady departed from Martin before he met with Jazz, then it is unlikely she is the murderer."

I gave a small nod and whispered, "And she'd have a lot less work to do if Martin was alive. I can't see her doing it. There doesn't seem to be any motive."

CHAPTER 17

t was just as well that Laura went when she did. The tearoom started to fill up again, and I was far too busy to think of further investigations.

Then, as luck would have it, Holly came into the kitchen as I was preparing an order. "I thought I'd drop in and see how Alan's getting on," she said. "Any chance of a cup of tea, too?"

I picked up a small teapot, spooned in some tea leaves, and headed for the water boiler.

"Alan? He's great. He's ever so good at dealing with the customers: he seems to be able to anticipate their every need. And he's an excellent Mr Bennet. Very funny."

"Anticipate their every need?" Mr. Wickers piped up, floating over. "That man's practically telepathic."

I had to agree.

Holly continued, oblivious to Mr Wickers. "He comes into the craft shop sometimes: he's a bit of an artist. I saw some of his artwork on display at the Sidmouth art club exhibition; it's very good. Perhaps you could get him to draw some of the customers."

Now that was something Alan hadn't mentioned when he came for his interview.

"An artist, is he?" Mr. Wickers said. "Admirable. Well, I hope he's better with a pencil than I was. My sketches were shocking."

"It's all down to practice," Lady Camilla commented. "You'd have been a great proficient if you'd only practiced."

"I'm glad you've popped in, Holly. I've got a question for you. What do you know about Martin Hawthorne's love life?" I asked.

"Martin's? Well, a fair bit, because he was quite open about it. He had lots of women on the go, and he never hid the fact. If anything, he made a point of telling his girlfriends that he was seeing other people. It seemed to make them more determined; they wanted to snare him and get to be the only one. Never happened, though."

"That reminds me of the late Lord Bath. He had wifelets, didn't he?"

Holly laughed. "Martin wasn't a lord, not by any stretch of the imagination, but he had the equivalent of wifelets. He was seeing quite a few women around the town, and further afield."

I goggled at her. "And they all knew about each other?"

"That's what I said." Holly looked slightly put out.

"It's not that I don't believe you, Holly. You're my best friend. It's just … why would a woman put up with that? I mean, what did Martin have going for him, other than a bit of fame decades ago?"

Holly shrugged. "Some women are very strange."

"Do you know the names of any of these girlfriends?"

"Not all of them, but a few."

"Go on."

"I saw Sophie Baker with him, and also Ellie Harris. I heard, although I can't confirm, that Sheila Clarke was seeing him, too."

My eyes widened. "Sheila Clarke? Really?" Sheila was the headteacher of the primary school. "Do you think one of them might have killed him?"

"I've thought about it," Holly replied, "but I don't know. Maybe one of them had more of an axe to grind, but that's speculation. And he might have been seeing someone else, too, but that's just a rumour."

I mused, "Sheila's a friend of my Aunt Ruby."

Holly grinned. "She'll be able to tell you more, then."

"Three girlfriends, possibly four. It's a wonder he had time to do anything else." I grinned back at Holly. "Maybe that's why he was tired at the committee meeting. He wasn't burning the candle at both ends – he was setting the whole thing on fire!"

"Talking of fire, how is the spark between you and O'Malley?"

I felt myself blush a little. Holly saw it.

"Not burning as bright as I'd hoped, but I suppose another murder doesn't help. Things keep getting in the way."

"Well, once you've solved the murder, that will leave you both free for a date. Then you'll be able to spend quality time with him, instead of in an interview room giving a witness statement."

"How did you know about that?" I couldn't remember telling Holly.

Then I realised. "Francis."

"Francis," we said it at the same time and laughed.

"It was hardly romantic," I said. "But I didn't mind being in a confined space with him.

Holly left shortly after, and I made a mental note to call Aunt Ruby. She was on holiday in Spain with a friend so I couldn't drop round her house like I usually did.

CHAPTER 18

I waited until I got home, then sat on the sofa and made a video call to Aunt Ruby. I wanted to see her reactions.

The ghosts and Wentworth gathered around as I dialed.

She picked up the call quickly. "Hello, darling, how are you? Is everything all right?"

The screen changed to show Aunt Ruby in sunglasses and sunhat, relaxing on a beach recliner.

"Everything's fine here. Well, sort of. I'm okay and Francis is, too. How is the holiday?"

"Divine. *España esta muy bella.*"

I had no idea what she was saying, but it sounded good.

"Have you heard the news about Martin Hawthorne? The guy who runs the folk festival?"

"Yes, of course, dear. I might be in Spain, but I still have my finger on the pulse of the town gossip. Nothing happens without me knowing about it, even if I am away. Why do you ask? Are you investigating again, or are you leaving it to that dishy Irish policeman?"

I should be leaving it to O'Malley, but I wanted to find out who would have the gumption to kill Martin. I didn't answer

Aunt Ruby's question, maybe because I didn't want to admit it to myself.

"How much do you know about Martin's relationships with women?" I asked, hoping to distract her.

"Well, he was a philanderer, that's for sure."

"I heard your friend Sheila was involved with him."

"Sheila?" Aunt Ruby laughed. "Oh yes, she was, but she's involved with everyone."

"She is?"

"You can ask her yourself: she's here with me." The video picture blurred as Aunt Ruby handed the phone to Sheila.

Mr Wickers sniggered. "Whoops."

I gave him a meaningful stare.

"Hello, dear," said Sheila. "What was it you wanted?" She also wore sunglasses, but she had a chiffon scarf draped around her face and wore bright-red lipstick.

"Er, hi, Sheila." I wished the ground would swallow me up.

"You wanted to know about me and Martin?"

"Er, yes," I muttered. In the little corner square, I could see that my face was bright pink.

"There's not much to say, dear. Of course I'm devastated that he's been murdered, but the reality is that I ditched him months ago. I didn't mind it being a casual relationship, but it was getting ridiculous. I'd have to book our dates two or three months in advance. So I ended it."

"Okay…" I couldn't believe what I was about to ask. "Do you know whether any of his other girlfriends might have had a reason to kill him?"

I heard Aunt Ruby say, "I knew you were looking into it!"

I sighed. "All right, I am looking into it."

"Good girl," said Aunt Ruby.

Sheila winked at me. "I've never contacted any of his other women. We all knew about each other, but we never spoke. Didn't want to rock the boat. None of us wanted to find out something we didn't want to know. Things went swimmingly as they were. Except for the fact I could hardly ever see him."

I heard Lady Camilla tut. Her expression showing her clear disdain of such behaviour.

"Are you sure none of his girlfriends got jealous?"

"We all thought the world of Martin, but he always made it clear he preferred being unattached, unmarried, independent, whatever you want to call it. He was great fun, though. Loved to party, and great at dancing the salsa. Those hips!"

I tried not to visualise it.

"Can you think of any reason why Martin might have been killed?"

"I couldn't say. He was a little touchy at times, but he had a good heart. Shame. Do find out who did it, Trinity. I was rather fond of him."

"I will, and thanks, Sheila. Enjoy your holiday. Bye, Aunt Ruby."

"Bye, darling," I heard Aunt Ruby say.

I ended the call.

"That didn't help much," said Lady Camilla. "The list of ladies this gentleman was courting seems a lot longer than we thought. Do you think it is worth tracing them all?"

I sighed. "If we could find out more about his movements that night, we might. For now, I'll make a note of the women he was involved with, and see if anything suspicious comes up about them."

Lady Camilla nodded her approval.

I picked up my phone and sent Holly a message, updating her, and listing all the women I knew about.

She replied a few minutes later with another two names.

CHAPTER 19

The next two days passed quickly and without any developments in Martin's murder.

Alan had agreed to work full time in the tearoom leading up to and through the folk festival, and I had to admit, having an extra pair of hands around was useful.

He'd learnt the ropes quickly, and it felt like he'd been around for a long time, not a few days.

When we'd finished for the evening, Alan, Carole, and Emma all came with me to Blackmore Gardens for the official opening of the festival. The usually quiet gardens had been transformed into another festival hub with a marquee in the middle, fitted with a wooden floor for ceilidhs and country dances.

The ghosts were with me, too, and they disappeared among the throng of the crowd as soon as I entered.

Around the perimeter of the gardens were the street food vendors' tents and stalls. On offer were bao buns and dumplings, burgers and hot dogs, Turkish kebabs and Thai food. The delicious smells made my stomach rumble.

Alan and Carole went to order some food; Emma spotted a friend and disappeared, too. I walked along, browsing the wide variety of merchandise on sale. I paused at a stall selling crystals. Now that I had located the enchanted moonstone, I didn't need to search every shop and stall. But I wanted to look anyway.

The stallholder was busy arranging one of the displays. I pressed the turquoise stone on my ring, summoning them, then whispered to the ghosts, "Come and have a look at these stones."

They floated over and looked over the stones. "A good variety here," Mr Wickers observed.

As the ghosts inspected the stones, I browsed. There was an array of jewellery: earrings, pendants, bracelets, and small wooden bowls full of small individual gemstones. On another table was a huge amethyst geode, with a sign that said "Not For Sale". It seemed to emanate a positive vibe.

"Looking for anything in particular?" the stall owner asked. She was at least seventy and dressed in black dungarees.

"Just browsing, really. Do you know anything about enchanted moonstones?"

The woman nodded in a knowing manner. "Not many of those about these days. Haven't seen one for years."

"Have you ever owned one?"

"Oh yes, and it definitely had magical powers. They say often there's a spirit inside one, but that's probably an old wives' tale."

"Where did you get yours from?"

The woman gave me a crafty look. "I do believe I've forgotten. And the only person I know who had any enchanted moonstones passed away a few years ago."

I sighed. "Thanks, anyway."

I browsed some of the other stones, and my eyes fell on a small deep-amber citrine stone, and I read the description: *Citrine is often called the "stone of abundance" or "success stone" and is believed to attract wealth, prosperity, and positivity.*

I bought it and put it in my pocket. I hoped it would bring me good luck.

The gardens were heaving now, but as I was taller than the average woman, I could still see most of what was going on. People were heading towards the main marquee, so I followed.

Inside, Laura was standing on the stage near the microphone, talking with some of the local dignitaries. I took up a position at the back of the marquee.

I looked around for the ghosts but couldn't see them. I thought I caught a glimpse of Lily, but when I looked again, she had gone.

Eventually, the opening ceremony began, and Laura stepped up to the microphone; her heels clicked softly against the wooden stage. Dressed in a fitted navy blazer over a floral blouse, her hair neatly pinned back, she paused for a moment, scanned the crowd, and waited until the noise level dropped.

"Welcome, everyone," she began. "Thank you for joining us today for this year's festival. Before we officially begin, I'd like to ask you all to join me in a moment of silence to remember Martin, whose dedication and spirit made this event possible for so many years."

A hush fell over the crowd, the lively buzz of conversation replaced by a solemn stillness. Some bowed their heads, while others gazed thoughtfully toward the stage.

After a long, respectful pause, Laura lifted her head. "Thank you," she said, her tone softening as she smiled faintly. "Martin would be proud to see all of you here, keeping this wonderful tradition alive. He loved this festival, and he'd be glad we're continuing without him. And now, without further ado, I declare this year's festival open!"

There was polite applause, most people seemingly not wanting to make a spectacle after such a solemn moment. Laura stepped back from the microphone, visibly relieved.

I had expected something a bit more ceremonial – perhaps the cutting of a ribbon, or a countdown. I'd never attended the opening before, not even as a child. Maybe Martin had been planning something Laura didn't know about.

Laura disappeared offstage. *Is that it?* I thought, underwhelmed.

I jumped as someone murmured in my ear. I heard the word "ceremony", but not much else. And I thought I recognised the voice. I did recognise the Irish accent.

I whipped around and let out a breath, my heart skipping. It was O'Malley.

He was dressed in his usual smart navy three-piece suit, looking immaculate. He must be on duty; he always seemed to be.

Heat rose to my face. "Oh, hi, there. What did you say?" I tried to sound casual.

O'Malley raised an eyebrow, his expression amused. "I said, is there more to this opening ceremony, or is that all there is?" He gestured loosely toward the stage. "I was expecting something with a bit more of a bang. Especially with the big lead-up."

"No, that's pretty much it. They keep it short and sweet."

"Short, yes. Sweet? Debatable." He glanced around the crowd. "I take it this isn't exactly the highlight of the festival?"

I shrugged, still acutely aware of his presence, the way he seemed to fill the space around him. "Not usually. Things pick up once the dancing starts. You'll see."

His gaze lingered on me for a moment longer than I expected, and it made my pulse quicken. "I'll hold you to that. So, are you going to the Regency dance workshop?"

"Is that part of the festival?"

"Yes, I saw it in the programme."

"I've only glanced at it so far. Is the Regency dance anything to do with folk?"

His smile broadened. "Clearly it must be, if it's in the programme."

"I'll have to check that out, then – if I have time. It's going to be very busy this week."

"Same here."

"I'm going to get something to eat. Care to join me?"

"I'd love to, but I'd better get going. It's my turn to look after the kids, and it's nearly time to pick them up."

I nodded. "Well, I'll see you around."

"Don't get into too much trouble while I'm gone. I'd hate to have to file a report on you, stealing the spotlight."

I smiled and felt myself go red.

O'Malley left, and I joined the queue for Thai food. I ordered Thai green curry, with jasmine rice and a vegetable spring roll. I took my food to a bench and tucked in, watching people mill about. After a few minutes, the gardens started to clear a little; some people were already going home. Others went into the marquee for a ceilidh. I wondered where the ghosts had got to and almost pressed the stone. Then Mr Darby floated up to me, weaving between groups of people who were stood, chatting on the paths. "I have just seen that young lady: Jazz, the musician. She is speaking with Danny Vance."

Of course he'd caught me with a mouthful of food. I held up my hand as I chewed frantically. "Really?" I said, at last. "What are they saying?"

"I couldn't hear. They began walking towards the town centre, and of course, I can't follow." He indicated the turquoise ring on my finger that held him back from going too far.

I still had half my food left, and it was delicious. I sighed and closed the lid. "Let's go." I walked towards the rear entrance of the gardens, which was closest to the town. The other ghosts floated over and fell in.

Guided by Mr Darby, I walked past the cemetery and the church to the town square.

"They are heading for the seafront," said Mr Darby, floating just ahead and above me.

But well before the seafront, they turned into a pub, Dukes. The place had a mix of styles, somewhere between a trendy gastropub and a classic seaside inn. There was a large outside terrace which was heaving. They went inside. The main room was bright and airy, with large windows letting in the early evening light and a polished wooden bar that stretched along one wall. It was the kind of place where locals mingled with tourists, drawn in by the inviting atmosphere and the promise of a good pint.

I followed them in, keeping my distance, and watched as they chose a table tucked into a quiet corner near the back. It wasn't hidden exactly, but far enough from the bar and the main foot traffic that they wouldn't draw attention. They sat close together, leaning in as they talked, their voices low.

I hung around nearby, looking at the menu, so that the ghosts could listen in to their conversation.

"They're discussing what to drink," Mr Darby reported. "They will order using a mobile telephone."

I saw Danny tap on his phone a few times, then put it on the table. He sat back and smiled at Jazz. Then he leaned forward again.

"He's telling her that he will take over mentoring her," said Mr Darby. I saw Jazz lean in. "Now Jazz is saying that he owes it to her to help."

"Really? That's a strange thing to say. Why would Danny owe her anything?"

Mr Wickers floated over to me. "Because she murdered Martin for him. It's obvious."

I raised my eyebrows. "Is it? She's small. And young. And it's against her interests to kill Martin. We agreed that, remember?"

Mr Darby pondered for a moment. "It is unusual for a young woman to murder, but not unheard of. Martin was killed by a blunt instrument to the head. Even a petite young lady like Jazz could kill with such an instrument."

I shook my head, unconvinced. "Whatever Danny owes her, I'm sure it's not because she killed Martin. But it is strange." I glanced over to their table, where Jazz was leaning forward, her hands moving animatedly as she spoke. Danny watched her with a faint smile, nodding along, clearly captivated by whatever she was saying. "What are they talking about now?"

"She was saying how much she loves writing songs and performing on stage. Now he's talking about all the ways he can help her," said Mr. Darby, his voice dry. "Apparently, he has lots of industry contacts."

"They're not mentioning Martin at all?"

"No."

How disappointing. I hoped they'd been discussing how one or both of them had murdered Martin.

Jazz laughed at something Danny said, her laughter light and musical. The way he leaned in closer made it clear he was playing the role of the charming mentor, but I wasn't the only one finding it hard to believe his motives were entirely professional.

The arrival of Danny's girlfriend, Denise, shattered whatever cosy dynamic they'd built at the table. She strode in past me, not even seeing me. She had purpose, her face set in a tight, unhappy line. Jazz froze mid-sentence as the girlfriend's eyes landed on her. From the corner of the room, I could hear snippets of her raised voice.

Jazz's face turned pink, and she shrank back slightly in her chair, fiddling with her bracelet. Danny, to his credit, looked mildly mortified, but not nearly apologetic enough.

"Not impressed, is she?" I muttered.

"Hardly," Mr. Darby replied. "The poor girl looks like she wants to disappear into the table."

In the end, they didn't linger. Danny barely finished his drink before his girlfriend marched them out, and Jazz followed a moment later, her expression carefully neutral but her shoulders tense. I watched them go, the whole scene leaving a strange unease in its wake.

CHAPTER 20

The following day, things kicked off in the tearoom.

In a good way.

While the other café and restaurant owners had warned me that my tearoom would be busy during the festival, I had underestimated the extent of that. I wasn't complaining, of course, but once the festival had begun, customers kept me occupied from the moment I opened right up to closing time. I even opened an hour earlier and closed an hour later, and still more customers kept arriving.

Just when I thought things couldn't get any more hectic, a group of morris dancers burst through the door, bells jingling. Dressed in Cotswold morris outfits, with white shirts and trousers and a bright green sash slung from shoulder to hip, they looked quintessentially English.

Their leader, a portly man with a huge handlebar mustache, approached me, his face flushed. "Can you fit us in? We're gasping for some tea and scones. We've been dancing for hours."

"Er, I think so. How many of you are there?"

"Fourteen."

"Come this way." I led them to the back of the tearoom and pulled three tables together.

I watched in amusement as they trooped through and sat down. One dancer, trying to manoeuvre between tables, accidentally hooked his bell-covered shin on a chair and the others cheered as he nearly fell over. "Come on, Dave, behave yourself!" one of them shouted.

I wondered what I had let myself in for.

By the time I got back round to their table, they'd polished off two scones each, and what seemed like endless tea. They also seemed much calmer: Alan's ability to look after people and soothe them clearly worked on morris dancers, too.

After closing, Carole and I rushed to the Methodist Church hall for the Regency dance workshop. It was the venue where I'd attended the festival committee meeting on the night Martin Hawthorne died. I'd thought about changing clothes first, then decided it would make the experience more authentic if I went in costume. Carole did the same. I also hoped that it would help me forget about the role the church hall might have played in Martin's murder.

As we entered the hall, a number of people were milling about.

The ghosts were next to me, and Lily clapped her hands. "I can't wait to dance!"

I wasn't sure which of the people was the instructor, until a woman in her sixties with short grey hair, dressed in jeans and a festival T-shirt, came over, smiling. "I'm Sue, the instructor." She looked me up and down. "Don't you look lovely. I take it you're a fan of all things Regency?"

I laughed. "You could say that. I run the Regency Tearoom on the seafront."

Sue's smile widened. "Oh yes, I've heard about it. I'm hoping to pop in soon."

"You'll be very welcomed."

Lady Camilla looked Sue up and down. "She should be in costume."

Sue looked at her watch, then turned to face the room. "Right, everyone!" she called. "I'm Sue. Gather round, and let's get dancing!"

Everyone crowded around Sue.

"We'll try a number of wonderful dances." She clapped her hands together. "The first dance we'll learn is The Shrewsbury Lasses. Those of you who've watched the 1995 version of *Pride and Prejudice* will remember it as Darcy and Elizabeth's dance at the Netherfield Ball!"

I knew it, of course: it was iconic. Jennifer Ehle and Colin Firth, dancing together, with lots of charged looks and tension.

"This is wonderful!" Lily clapped her hands. "I remember this as though it were yesterday! Who will dance with me?" She looked at Mr Wickers, then at Mr Darby, but didn't even glance at Mr Collingwood.

"I'll dance with you, of course," said Mr Wickers. He held out his hand. Lily took it, and they floated to the side of the room to await the start of the dancing.

Mr Collingwood started to ask Lady Camilla, "I would be equally honoured if Your Ladyship—"

But she cut him off before he could finish. "I'm too old to dance."

Mr Darby disappeared through a wall, clearly wishing to amuse himself somewhere else.

I did a quick headcount: about twenty people, with slightly fewer men than women. Being tall, I would usually have been asked to dance as a man, to even things up, but my Regency dress made that impossible. I smiled to myself; that was a good move.

The two musicians, who had been sitting patiently at the side of the room, came to life as soon as the signal was given.

The fiddle player launched into the lively, lilting tune, the melody bright. The pianist followed.

The music was unmistakably Regency: an elegant country dance tune, light yet structured, with a natural ebb and flow that mirrored the movements we were about to attempt. It was the kind of music that made you feel as though you'd stepped into a Jane Austen novel, full of charm, grace, and just a touch of flirtation.

I tried to concentrate on my own steps, but I made several mistakes because I couldn't help watching Lily and Mr Wickers. They were enchanting together.

My partner was a man called Nigel. He was tall and lean, with silver hair combed back, dressed in light-tan trousers, and a smart black T-shirt. He had a stern, schoolmasterly air about him, due to his upright posture. He gave me disapproving glances every time I went wrong. I returned a weak smile and wished that I was dancing with O'Malley instead. He would have held my attention, I was sure. But I supposed that when O'Malley wasn't solving murders he needed time with his children.

Half an hour later, we'd practised the dance a few times and were getting quite good. Sue called a short break. I went to the side of the room and joined the drinks queue.

"Have you heard?" said a woman in line behind me. "There's been another attack. On the other member of Velvet Vortex."

My ears pricked up. "I hadn't, no," said another woman. "What's the guy's name?"

I turned. "Danny Vance?"

Both the women looked at me. "That's it. Danny Vance. He was in the group with Martin, years ago."

"What's happened?" I pressed, as we all shuffled forward.

"Well, last night *he* was attacked, too," said the first woman. Someone bashed him on the head, just like Martin."

"That's terrible!" I exclaimed. "Is he dead?"

"No, luckily. He was hit over the head, like Martin, but he survived. I heard from my next door neighbour, who works there, they've moved him to the Sidmouth Community Hospital for observation."

My mind whirled. Danny had been my prime suspect, but now he'd been attacked, as well.

The second woman looked thoughtful. "Maybe it's a disgruntled fan from all those years ago, when they were famous."

"Possibly," I replied. "But they must have known lots of people since then."

The line moved forward again, and I remembered where I was. I recalled the moment when Danny had strolled into the committee meeting in this very room and the expression on Martin's face.

"When did the attack happen?" I asked.

"Last night. I'm not sure where, though."

Sue clapped her hands, making me jump. "Five minutes, everyone, five minutes and we're back dancing."

Five minutes later, and my mind was full of the attack, so I kept making mistakes and had to apologize to Nigel several times. He wasn't happy with me.

In the end, I asked to swap with Carole's partner, and Nigel readily agreed. By the time the workshop finished, I was determined to visit Danny in hospital.

CHAPTER 21

The community hospital was in the centre of Sidmouth, just a short walk away from the workshop venue and next to Blackmore Gardens.

I went in. The reception window had its blind pulled down, and a *RECEPTION CLOSED* sign was stuck on the window for good measure.

"I need your help," I said to the ghosts. "Can you go and find Danny for me?"

The ghosts nodded and disappeared down the corridor.

Left alone, I looked around and saw a CCTV camera in the corner. I would look like a complete nutter if anyone ever checked that footage.

I didn't have to wait long. A minute later, Mr Collingwood reappeared. "We have found the gentleman in question."

"Lead the way."

I followed him down the long corridor and round the corner to a door with a sign above that said Connaught Ward.

I pushed the door, but it was locked. Just my luck, though it was probably good for the patients' safety that not just anyone could walk in. I pressed the buzzer at the side of the door and waited.

Mr. Collingwood floated nearby, and after a couple of minutes, he disappeared through the locked door. A few seconds later, he stuck his head through it. "There is no nurse at the nursing station," he said, with a note of disdain.

"They must be on their rounds. How can I get in? Can't you do some juju and open the door?"

Mr. Collingwood shook his head. "This is a locked medical ward. I will not."

I sighed and pressed the buzzer again. This time, a nurse approached behind me.

She looked me up and down. No surprise as I was still in my Regency costume. "Yes?"

"I-I've come to see Danny Vance."

She looked at her watch. "There's only twenty minutes of visiting hours left."

"That's okay. I just wanted to check he's all right."

"You a relative?"

"Y-yes, I'm his niece," I lied.

The nurse opened the door fully and let me in.

"Thank you."

The ghosts followed close behind, except for Mr Colling-wood, who indicated the way to Danny.

It was a small ward, with six beds in all. Two were empty, and in the far right-hand corner was Danny, watching something on an iPad. He was dressed in a hospital gown, with a large bandage around his head.

He looked up when I approached. His eyes were half-closed, and I guessed that he'd been given strong painkillers.

"Hello, Danny. Do you remember me?"

He shifted against his pillows and blinked a few times. "Am I in one of those costume dramas? Did they send you to cheer me up with period reenactments?"

I sat on the chair next to his bed, settling my skirts.

"Don't stand on ceremony," he said, sitting up a little.

I ignored his sarcastic comment. "How are you doing?"

"I was whacked over the head by some maniac. How do you think I'm doing?"

"That must have been awful."

"It was. But even though someone's tried to kill me, the police are doing nothing. For all I know, they could come in here and have another go." He stared at me, and I realised that he was probably wondering whether I was the guilty party.

"You've given a statement?"

"Of course I have."

"You're quite safe here. For one thing, the door's locked."

"How did you get in, then?"

"Er, a nurse let me in. You don't need to worry. I'm not here to kill you. I'm trying to find out who is behind it."

"Yeah? Well, good luck with that. The police have been useless."

I thought about O'Malley. He wasn't useless. He was intuitive, sharp, and thorough, never one to let a detail slip by. However, I decided not to contradict Danny's opinion. I wanted him on my side.

"Can you tell me what happened?" I asked. "What do you remember?"

"I was walking along the esplanade last night, turned down a side road, and that's all I can remember. I woke up in A and E in Exeter."

"What time was it when you got hit?"

He thought for a moment. "Not too late, about eleven."

"Who were you with?"

"I was on my own."

That was strange, since I'd seen him in the pub with Jazz and then his girlfriend, Denise, that night. Obviously, I couldn't admit I'd been following him, though.

"And you didn't see anyone behind you?"

He shook his head a little, then winced. "Whoever it was

must have been light on their feet because I never heard a thing."

"I wonder if they have CCTV in that area?" I mused.

"The police are checking that, they say. The only thing they *are* doing."

I made a mental note to call O'Malley to find out.

Mr Darby had been floating at the end of the bed and said, "Ask him if he saw anyone he knew before the attack."

I did as he suggested. "Did you see anyone you knew just before the attack?"

"Nah, apart from that Jazz girl. She wants me to mentor her. We'd had a chat earlier that night, and then she went out on the esplanade busking afterwards. I stopped to listen. She's got talent, you know."

How strange, I thought. Jazz had been with Martin just before he'd been murdered, too.

"Very suspicious," Mr Darby commented.

"So she had her guitar with her?"

"Yeah, and an amp."

So it couldn't have been Jazz: she would have had to leave all her gear unattended on the seafront to follow and attack Danny. If she had her guitar and amp with her, there's no way she could have silently approached Danny and hit him. And again, why would she want to kill someone who'd agreed to mentor her?

"Who do you think might want to attack both you and Martin?"

Danny shrugged.

"A crazed fan?"

He barked out a bitter laugh. "Truth is, we haven't had any of those for decades. Oh, we had plenty back in the day, and there are still lots of fans who get nostalgic over us, but that's it. All our fans from back then are in their forties or fifties, or even older. They're not crazed – they're more likely to be comparing HRT tablets. No offence," he added as an afterthought, and I wondered how much the painkillers were adding to his loose tongue. When I'd spoken to him previously, he'd been brash, but not so rude and forthright like now.

"There must be a connection, though. It can't be random that someone has attacked you and Martin within days of each other."

A sudden thought struck me. What if this a red herring? What if Danny had staged an attack, but it was a cover, to make it look as if someone was after them both? That would deflect suspicion from him, and he was the prime suspect so far. If that were true, it was an elaborate and somewhat dangerous way to cover up the fact that he'd murdered his ex-bandmate.

I would definitely have to ask O'Malley about that. Without seeing Danny's medical records, which no doubt would be on the computer, there was no way of knowing how bad his injury was.

Then I looked at how pale Danny was. What was I thinking? Who would get themselves hit over the head to try and deflect suspicion? No one would do a convincing job of that. That was a very dangerous way to do it. Unless he got someone else to do it for him.

"Doctors said I was lucky to survive," said Danny, who had caught me staring. "Any harder, and it could've been much worse. I could have ended up like Martin."

I shook my head in disbelief. "Is there anything I can get you?"

"Thanks, but no. Denise is out getting me some provisions. The food here's just as I expected: disgusting."

"Tomorrow morning, I'll bring you some fresh scones." I stood up and said my goodbyes, not knowing what else to say.

Outside, I discussed what we'd heard with the ghosts.

"You thought he might have staged the attack," said Lady Camilla.

I gaped at her. "Are you a mind reader?"

"No, but I thought it, too."

"I can't see Danny arranging a hit – that's just ridiculous. But if not, who else would want to kill both members of Velvet Vortex?

CHAPTER 22

The next morning, as promised, I made my way back to the hospital with a box of scones, Devon clotted cream, and strawberry jam for Danny.

I made my way back to Danny's ward. This time there were plenty of nurses to let me in. Danny wasn't at his bed; he'd been taken for a scan. So I left the box on his side table, with a note, and left.

I was just leaving the building, when who should I see coming in? O'Malley.

That caught me off-guard. I wasn't expecting to see him.

"DI Handsome!" Lily exclaimed, and spun high into the air like a cyclone.

"Hello," I said nonchalantly and tried to ignore Lily.

"Are you here for a social call, or are you sick?" He frowned in concern.

Out of the corner of my eye, I saw Lily float back down to listen in.

"Social call. I promised Danny I'd bring him some scones."

"Thoughtful."

"Well, I heard about what happened to him, and wanted

to help. There's nothing like scones and clotted cream to make you feel better, and he said the food wasn't good in the hospital."

O'Malley paused for a moment. "You're not trying to find the killer yourself, are you?"

"Me?" I feigned innocence.

"I'm just doing my bit to help a man who's been the victim of a vicious attack."

"He doesn't believe you." Lily giggled.

I glanced at Lily, then found myself saying, "But it's no coincidence that both Danny and Martin were attacked in a similar way, and both of them were in a band together back in the day. Don't you think?"

O'Malley crossed his arms. A faint smile in his lips. "Are you probing to see whether I'm doing my job properly?"

"No, no. Just thinking out loud. It just seems to me that someone has it in for the band. Even though they split up decades ago."

"We're working on it. But you know how these things go – takes time to get all the pieces to fit." He leaned in slightly, his voice dropping. "Leave the investigating to me, all right? I don't need to be worrying about you stumbling into trouble like last time."

Lily whispered with a dreamy sigh. "Such a hero. Putting your safety first."

I rolled my eyes at her and managed a small smile for O'Malley. "Of course. I'll leave it to the professionals."

O'Malley uncrossed his arms and smiled. "I'll be seeing you soon."

"I'll hold you to that."

———

I opened the tearoom early again, and by ten o'clock, the tearoom was half-full. It seemed that the festival goers wanted tea and scones for breakfast. If I'd thought about it sooner, I would have devised a brunch menu, but it was too late for that now. Next year, I'd be more prepared.

The doorbell had tinkled at intervals all day, announcing yet more customers to partake of my wares. But partway through the afternoon, I looked up from the tray of scones I'd been arranging to see the familiar face of my cousin Francis. He was out of uniform, and accompanied by a woman of a similar age whom I didn't recognise. She was late twenties, dressed in a flowery summer dress, with wavy blonde hair that framed a heart-shaped face. "Francis!" I made my way over, curious to meet his companion.

Francis blushed and ran his hand through his hair. I looked expectantly at his companion. Francis swallowed. "Um ...this is my..." He hesitated for a moment. "This is Chloe."

She was dressed in a white T-shirt and black shorts, and her hair was in a messy bun, with a few loose strands framing her face.

Luckily, there was a cosy table free in the corner, and I took them to it. They looked as if they needed some time alone because they both looked nervous in a first-date sort of way.

"I really like your tearoom," said Chloe.

"Thank you." I handed her a menu. Then I leaned towards Francis. "How is the murder investigation going?" I murmured.

"Good, as far as I know. There's been talk about it all over town."

"Really? What have you heard?"

"Everyone in Sidmouth seems to have a theory about Martin's death. And each one's more outlandish than the last." He chuckled and looked at Chloe.

"Are they all outlandish?"

"Well, there's a rumour about Laura. You know, the one who runs the folk festival now."

I nodded, pulled up a chair and sat down. "What about her?"

"Well…" He leaned in and lowered his voice. "According to Gail, who works at the council offices, her husband's electrician's aunt said there was a to-do between Laura and Martin just days before his murder."

I leaned in, too. "What kind of to-do?"

"Apparently Martin was planning to sack Laura."

My eyebrows shot up. "Sack Laura? But why? I thought Martin had been training her to take over from him, for years. Why would he sack her now?"

"Gail said he'd found out she was planning to modernise the festival too much. I'm not sure how, but he didn't like it."

"You don't know what he objected to?"

Francis shrugged. "Nope. But the argument was big enough for O'Malley to investigate it now Martin's been murdered."

I wanted to know more. "What was the date of the to-do?"

"It was a couple of days before he was killed."

That meant it was after the committee meeting. I hadn't noticed any animosity between Martin and Laura then, so whatever it was, it must have blown up afterwards.

"I didn't attend, but PC Sutton did. She said a disturbance was reported in Martin's flat in the early evening by a neighbour. People shouting and there was banging, too. She said when she arrived, things had calmed down. Laura was there, and they both looked flustered but each claimed they'd just had a disagreement. I think they were shocked someone had called the police."

I felt a pang of jealousy that Francis had managed to find that out and jumped ahead of me. Why did I feel like that? I had a busy tearoom to run, and no time to be investigating a murder.

And besides, Laura had always seemed so passionate about the folk festival, even in the short time that I'd known her. If she was planning to modernise it, then it can't have been a bad thing.

"So O'Malley thinks it's suspicious?"

Francis shrugged. "Martin was murdered just days later. He's following up on everything."

"It certainly needs looking into."

My thoughts were interrupted by the chime of the shop bell signalling another arrival. Then my heart skipped a beat as Laura herself came in.

CHAPTER 23

Laura gazed around her as though looking for something – or someone. Then I stood up, and our eyes locked. She managed a small smile and made her way over to me. "Trinity, do you have a moment? There's something I need to talk to you about." A tiny pause. "It's about the festival."

I glanced at Francis, who was watching us with interest. While I was grateful for his previous sharing of information, I didn't want whatever Laura told me to become common knowledge in Sidmouth. "Of course, Laura. Why don't we step into the kitchen for a bit of privacy?"

Once we were in the kitchen, Laura spoke. "I'm having a lot of trouble with Gordon, the crêpe stall man. He's been hassling me almost nonstop: asking me to move his pitch to his old spot near the main marquee."

"Oh yes, he told me all about it the other day. He and Martin had a disagreement over his pitch, didn't they?"

Laura huffed. "Apparently so, and now, even though the festival has already started, he wants me to organise getting his pitch moved."

"What will you do?"

"I can't move him, can I? The ticket booth is where his old pitch used to be. All the other prime pitches have been taken, and contracts have been signed. I can't back out of those: it would be a legal nightmare."

I nodded in sympathy, while scrutinising Laura. I couldn't imagine her killing Martin. She seemed so ... ordinary. Then I jumped as someone spoke in my ear. "Ask her about being sacked by Martin."

I turned slightly and saw Lily.

"So, Laura, I assume you haven't come here just to moan. Do you want me, as café and restaurant liaison, to have a word with him?"

Laura looked relieved. "Yes please, that's exactly it. Tell Gordon, if you wouldn't mind, that next year he will have his prime position back, but there's nothing I can do now."

"Okay. I'll go and talk to him if and when there's a lull in customers."

She put her hand on my arm. "You're wonderful, Trinity. Thank you."

I decided that it was now or never. "Laura... I've heard some talk around town about you and Martin. Specifically, about you having a disagreement before his death."

Laura's eyes widened. "What? What kind of talk?" There was a tremor in her voice.

I took a deep breath. "Well ... there's a rumour that Martin was planning to sack you from becoming festival organiser. Is that true?"

For a moment, Laura stared at me, seemingly frozen. Then she let out a bitter laugh. "Oh, is that what people are saying? I don't know why I'm surprised. This town loves gossip."

"Then it's not true?" I asked, feeling both relieved and confused.

Laura sighed. "It's complicated. Martin and I did have a disagreement, yes, but it wasn't about sacking me. I wanted to make some changes to the festival. Bring in more modern acts, expand the scope, that sort of thing. Martin was resistant to the idea. We argued, yes, but we were working towards a compromise. Especially as he was about to step down."

"So he wasn't going to sack you?"

"No, no, nothing like that," Laura said, shaking her head. "Martin could be difficult to work with, but he wasn't unreasonable. We were going to meet up after the festival to review it and hash out the arrangements for next year, but then…" Laura sniffed and wiped her eyes. "Oh, all this silly gossip… Trinity, people don't really believe I had something to do with Martin's death, do they?"

Now I felt guilty for mentioning it at all. "I'm sure most people don't, Laura. It's just idle speculation in a small town. People are shocked and they're looking for answers. Not necessarily in the right place."

"But why me?" Laura's voice rose slightly. "Is it so hard to believe that I could disagree with someone without resorting to murder? Honestly, I've poured my heart and soul into this festival for years. Of course, Martin and I had our differences, but I would never… I could never…" She covered her face and started to cry.

I put my arms around her. "Of course you wouldn't, Laura. I'm sorry for even bringing it up. We all know how much the festival means to you. Anyway, now I know the truth, I can help put the rumours to bed."

After a few moments, Laura moved away a little. I handed her a paper napkin and she wiped her eyes. "I'm sorry for falling apart like that," she said, her breath catching. "Everything's so stressful at the moment. It always is, during the festival, but I expected Martin to be here to help." She closed her eyes. "That sounds so selfish, doesn't it? Martin's been murdered, and all I talk about is how it's affected me."

"It's not selfish, Laura. This has left you in a difficult situation with lots more work to do. Isn't there anyone you can ask to help you?"

"Everyone's rallying round as best they can, but Sarah resigning when she did has piled even more work on my shoulders." She sighed. "I suppose at least I'll be prepared for the amount of work it will be next year. I'll make sure I have an assistant in place in good time."

Footsteps came closer, and Emma came in with a tray of dirty crockery. She glanced at Laura. "I'm sorry, am I interrupting you?"

Laura straightened up, the napkin balled in her hand. "No, no, I must be going. Thank you so much for offering to talk to Gordon, Trinity." She scurried out of the kitchen and was gone.

CHAPTER 24

The lull in customers I had hoped for didn't happen until gone four in the afternoon. I was pleased to have a busy tearoom, of course, but I also wanted to fulfil my promise to Laura.

At five past four I told my staff I was popping out for a little while and hurried along the esplanade to Gordon's crêpe stand Holy Crêpe. Even in that short distance, I passed people eating crêpes. Hopefully that meant Gordon's business hadn't been affected as much as he feared.

As I arrived at Gordon's stall, he was making a customer's order. He poured the batter onto the circular griddle, then used a metal flat device to spread it. Once it had solidified, he flipped the crêpe with a long, thin palette knife. Then the best bit – he put a huge blob of chocolate spread onto the crêpe. As it began to melt, he spread it over half the crêpe, folded and served it. The woman waiting could hardly wait to grab it and start eating.

Mr Wickers floated through the tent walls and looked around. "Bit messy behind here." He floated over to the cash tin and put his head inside it for a moment. "Goodness me, there is a lot of cash in here."

Then Gordon caught sight of me. "Trinity!" he exclaimed, beaming. "Are you here for a crêpe?"

"Not this time, Gordon, though they do look delicious. I've come in my role as the festival's café and restaurant liaison. Laura's asked me to talk to you—"

Gordon huffed. "That stupid woman! I thought Martin was bad as the festival director, but she's even worse."

I ignored that, keen to pass on my message and get back to work. "Laura's upset because you won't stop hassling her about the pitch. There's no point: there's nothing she can do about it now because all the contracts have been signed. But she asked me to promise on her behalf that next year you'll have prime position again."

Gordon's eyes narrowed. "Did she ask you to come?"

I stood my ground. "Yes, she did. It's my job on the festival committee. She's very upset because you won't leave her alone."

Gordon considered this, and seemed mollified, then huffed again. "That's all very well, but I'm still not happy. My takings are half what they were last year, you know."

"I understand, but Laura has promised. I'll hold her to it, too." I wasn't sure how I would do that, or indeed whether I would still be acting as liaison next year, but I decided to worry about that when the time came.

"I'll leave her be, then. For now. But once this festival's over, I'll be asking her to sign a contract for next year."

"Then I'll witness it."

A customer hovered nearby wanting to order a crêpe, so I said goodbye and walked away, followed by the ghosts.

"That appeared to go well," Lady Camilla observed.

"Yes, it did," I replied quietly so no one would overhear. "I just hope he keeps his word and stops bothering Laura."

Mr. Collingwood floated forward. "A gentleman should always keep his word. If not, his honour is at risk."

"Quite so," said Lady Camilla, and Mr Collingwood smiled at her gratefully.

I was almost back at the tearoom when I noticed a young woman hovering near the entrance: Jazz.

"Hello," I said.

Jazz's head jerked up and she stared at me.

"Would you like to come in? We're open later than usual, for the festival."

Jazz nodded and followed me in. "I was hoping to talk to you…"

I wasn't expecting that, but I smiled at her to try and put her at ease. "Take a seat over there. Now, what would you like? Tea and scones?"

Jazz nodded, looking grateful, and I returned as quickly as I could with a tray because I wanted to know what she could possibly want to talk to me about. I sat down opposite her. "So, Jazz, how can I help?"

Lady Camilla had been floating nearby. I couldn't ask what she was doing, but I gave her a meaningful look, and she answered. "I am simply observing. This Jazz gal looks like she needs some female companionship and guidance. Unfortunately I cannot give it."

Jazz watched as I poured two cups of tea. I handed one to her, and she wrapped her hands around it as if seeking comfort from its heat. "I…I heard you've been asking questions about Martin's death. About what happened that night."

My pulse quickened. "Yes, I have. I'm trying to understand. I was the one who found his body. It's been quite a shock to our community, not just me—"

"I was there,"Jazz blurted. She met my gaze. "That night, I mean. I think I was the last person to see Martin before…"

I knew this already. "Can you tell me what happened?"

"I met Martin that evening, because he wanted to discuss my performances at the festival. We met at the Anchor, had a couple of drinks, talked about music. He was... He was in a good mood, and excited about the festival."

"Am I right in thinking that he was mentoring you?"

"Well, he hadn't started, but he'd promised that he would."

I surveyed her, and thought perhaps Martin had other things on his mind besides mentoring when he made Jazz the offer. I glanced at Lady Camilla, and from her expression, she thought the same. But whatever his intention, I decided that it was all water under the bridge now. "What time did you leave the pub?"

"Around ten thirty, I think. Martin said he had one more thing to do before heading home." Jazz's voice quavered. "I never imagined... If I'd known…"

"You couldn't have known, Jazz. None of us could have predicted what would happen."

Jazz nodded, blinking back tears. "I know, but I can't help feeling... And with what happened to Danny—"

"You saw Danny before he was attacked, too?" I knew she had, but I wanted to hear what she would say.

"I... Yes, I did. I ran into him after the opening ceremony and we had a drink in Dukes." I knew she was telling the truth, but of course, I wasn't going to admit that I'd been following them.

"Jazz… Are you aware that people have been talking? You were seen with both Martin and Danny before they were attacked."

The young woman's face crumpled. "I know. I've heard the whispers and seen the looks. That's partly why I want to talk to you. I need you to know that I didn't hurt Danny or Martin. I would never! You believe me, don't you?"

I studied Jazz's face. Her distress appeared genuine, and I wanted to say that I believed her, but did I? Her presence on both nights was a compelling coincidence – if it *was* a coincidence.

"I'm a little confused... Why come to me?" I ventured.

"You know lots of people in the town. You seem so nice; I thought you'd be a good person to talk to and..." She hesitated as if struggling to get the words out. "I heard you're dating DI O'Malley."

I wasn't expecting that. Part of me felt pleased that people were gossiping about me and O'Malley. That they thought there was a "Trinity and O'Malley". I wanted there to be, but we weren't quite there yet. I could have denied it, but I didn't want to.

I felt a whoosh and a giggle, then Lily appeared behind Jazz. "Did someone mention DI Handsome?"

Lady Camilla tutted. "Shush, girl, they are talking about the murder case."

"Can you tell me more about the night Danny was attacked? When exactly did you and Danny part ways?"

Jazz closed her eyes as if trying to recall the details. "It was around eight thirty, I think."

"What did you talk about?" I knew some of it already, from the ghosts listening in, but I wanted her version.

"Just that Martin and I had met to discuss him mentoring me. Danny said he'd do it instead. We weren't talking for long because his girlfriend turned up and thought something was going on between us."

"And after that, what happened?"

"I went to my hotel room. I was tired, and I had an early rehearsal the next day." She leaned forward. "I swear, Trinity, I didn't hurt Danny. When I left him he was fine. I had no reason. He was about to help me."

I nodded slowly. "Did you see anyone else that night? In particular, was anyone acting suspiciously around Danny?" I hoped she hadn't spotted me.

"No. It was busy everywhere: the festival had just opened."

We sat in silence for a moment. She fiddled with necklace

around her neck. "I'm scared. With all the rumours going around, people are looking at me as if I'm the murderer. I thought that if I just kept my head down it would all blow over. Can you tell everyone it wasn't me?"

Now, here was a dilemma. I knew that I ought to believe Jazz. She was small: much smaller than the two men who had been attacked. She had no obvious motive: if anything, the attacks disadvantaged her. And most killers weren't young women in their early twenties. But something was stopping me from saying that I believed her.

"I'm glad you came to me," I said, slowly, as I searched for the right words. "But I have to ask... Is there anything else you can tell me? Anything that might help us understand what happened to Martin and Danny?"

Jazz chewed her bottom lip, her eyes full of doubt. "I... Well, there is one thing. It might be nothing, but it might make you think I did it."

"Go on." I sat forward.

"The night I met with Martin, at The Anchor, someone was watching us. A man, sitting in the corner. He kept glancing our way."

My interest was piqued. "Did you recognise him?"

"Yes. It was the man who runs the crêpe stall."

Gordon.

I heard Lady Camilla do a sort of gasp. "Ask her if Gordon left before or after them?"

"That's Gordon." There was no love lost between Martin and Gordon. Perhaps Gordon was glancing their way because of the crêpe pitch situation. "Did he leave before you and Martin?"

"No."

I sipped my tea, looking at Jazz over the rim of the cup. This was very interesting. "Thank you for coming to talk to me, Jazz. It must have been difficult with all the rumours flying around."

Jazz managed a small smile. "Thanks for listening. I was so afraid that everyone had already made up their minds that I'm guilty."

"Small towns can be quick to judge," I replied. "But they can also band together in times of trouble."

She nodded, her hands twitching slightly as if unsure what to do with them. "I should go. I've got to prepare for my next rehearsal. Thanks again, Trinity."

I watched her stand up. She was slow, as though she was reluctant to leave but couldn't think of a reason to stay. She paused by the door, glancing back at me, then left.

For a moment, I stayed seated, staring at the empty chair she'd left behind. She hadn't touched her scone and left most of the tea. Her distress had felt genuine, her fear palpable, and yet … something didn't seem right. Was it the coincidence of her presence at both incidents? Or was it something in her manner, the way her eyes darted away when she tried to recall details? She wanted me to believe her. But I only had her word for it.

The fact that she'd mentioned Gordon was in the pub the night was a revelation. He'd said he'd gone home, but if Jazz was telling the truth, Gordon had lied.

CHAPTER 25

That night, I collapsed on the sofa as soon as I got home. Wentworth jumped up for lots of attention. He'd clearly been missing me and the ghosts now that I was spending more time in the tearoom. Thank goodness the festival only lasted a week. If the tearoom was this busy all the time, I would have to recruit a manager.

I opened my eyes when the doorbell rang and jumped as I saw Mr. Wickers's face inches from mine. "You must wake up," he said. "DI Handsome is at the door."

"What?" I said, as I rubbed my eyes. I looked down: I was still wearing my Regency gown, and Wentworth was snuggled next to me.

"You fell asleep on the sofa and we didn't want to wake you. You looked so peaceful."

I sat up. "I was so tired." I yawned. "I still feel tired. What's the time?"

"Five minutes to eight," said Mr. Wickers, pointing at the clock.

The doorbell rang again.

"Coming!" I shouted. I stood up and checked myself in the mirror, smoothing my hair.

Lady Camilla looked me up and down and tutted. "You look as if you have just woken up."

I rolled my eyes. "I know, but I can't keep O'Malley waiting."

Lady Camilla looked down her nose at me. "Well, let us hope that he likes the wild look on a lady."

I went to the door and opened it. "Sorry about that. I fell asleep on the sofa."

Mr Darby cleared his throat behind me. "Yes, always best to tell the truth to a police officer."

O'Malley smiled. "Been burning the midnight oil?"

I opened the door wider to let him in. "No. I'm just very busy at work. Run off my feet, actually. I didn't realise how much the festival goers would like tea and scones. Not that I'm complaining."

He looked at me, his eyes hypnotic – or was it because I was still waking up from my nap and looked wild? "I came to see how you were; I wanted to see you. And I had an idea that you might be hungry, so I thought we could share this." He held up a takeaway bag. The aroma of delicious food hit my nose, and my stomach rumbled.

"Oh, wow! Thank you. And no, I haven't eaten yet. Come through to the kitchen."

He put the bag on the kitchen table while I fetched plates and cutlery.

"What would you like to drink?" I asked as I set down a plate in front of him. "I have beer, lemonade, tea, coffee, or tap water."

"Just water would be grand. I'm driving."

We sat in companionable silence as we ate the fish and chips. The ghosts floated in and out of the room, observing us, until I gave them a look they couldn't misinterpret. Lily grinned and said, "Have fun" before she dissipated.

"I had an interesting visitor in the tearoom today," I said, eventually.

"A Regency time traveller looking for a latte?" He smiled.

I tried not to laugh. "No, Jazz Thompson."

O'Malley raised his eyebrows but said nothing.

I finished my mouthful and put my fork down. "She wanted to talk to me because of all the rumours that are going around about her."

"What rumours are those?"

"You must have heard them?"

O'Malley put his knife and fork down.

"I'm sorry, I didn't mean it like that," I said, realising I'd said it a little too harshly. "I meant that, of course you know about the rumours, because that's your job."

"It is, but I rarely take notice of rumours. If you do, they can get you in trouble. My grandmother used to say, 'Don't let a whisper be the wind that steers your ship.'"

"Very wise. But some rumours are true."

"I prefer to deal with the facts."

"An admirable approach."

"What did Jazz say?" He picked up his knife and fork and started eating again.

"She told me about what happened on the nights when she was with Martin and Danny. Before they were attacked."

He smiled. "I've already spoken to her about it."

Of course he had. Had I expected anything less?

"I'm not sure why she'd speak to me, more than anyone else," I said. I didn't mention she thought O'Malley and I were a couple.

"Maybe it's because you're trying to find out who the murderer is. And you know most people in town, too."

I opened my mouth to protest, but he was right.

"She kept asking me if I believed her. It seemed really important to her."

O'Malley considered, "Strange. She wasn't like that with me."

"So why would she care if I think she's innocent? Surely it's more important that you think so."

"She probably knows you have lots of sway in the community. So if you believed her, everyone else would, too."

I wasn't sure about that. I did know a lot of people, and I'd grown up in Sidmouth, but I'd been away for years. Most of them have moved away or died. During that time, lots of new people had arrived, and others had moved away. I was still getting to know everyone.

"Did you believe her?" he asked.

I sat back in my chair and sighed. "I'm not sure. And I can't work out why. I mean, what motive would she have? She said Martin and then Danny had agreed to mentor her. Why would she risk that?"

"That's the conclusion I came to. Although Jazz had been with both men not long before they were attacked, she had no motive."

I pushed some food around my plate with my fork, contemplating. "She did mention that she saw Gordon in the pub the night she was with Martin. But Gordon told me he'd gone home after packing up for the night."

O'Malley's eyes narrowed. "When did he tell you that?"

"I introduced myself a couple of days after Martin was killed. It's part of my job on the committee. He mentioned it, though. Why would he lie?"

"Maybe he forgot to tell you."

"Did he tell you?"

"He did."

That deflated me. O'Malley was one step ahead of me again. I should be pleased.

"He said he stopped off for a pint before heading home. Nothing unusual in that."

"Except for the fact Gordon was not happy with Martin over the pitch situation. Did he tell you Martin wanted cash so Gordon could keep his pitch?"

"He did, yes. He was very vocal about it."

I sighed, then remembered: "Martin had a lot of girl-friends."

"He did. I'm not entirely sure I've tracked them all down, but they all have alibis."

"How many exactly do you know about? I know about five."

"Seven, so far."

"Seven!" I repeated in disbelief.

O'Malley chuckled. "I know. How he had time for every-thing, I'll never know."

I pushed my plate away. "So if it wasn't Jazz, Danny, Laura, or Gordon, who could it be?"

"I've not ruled out any of the last three. Not completely. They all have a motive, and shaky alibis. Although none of the motives are very strong. Most murders are crimes of passion or when something big is about to threaten the killer. That is the key to solving it." O'Malley finished the last of his fish and chips.

"There's always something more."

"I'm not supposed to be talking to you about this. And you're not supposed to be investigating either."

I pondered. "I'm hardly investigating. I'm too busy. But people talk to me. It's hard to ignore something so major that's happened in the town."

Our conversation was interrupted by Wentworth coming into the kitchen. He went straight over to O'Malley, pushed himself against his chair, waiting for him to pet him.

"Hello there, little fella." O'Malley reached down and stroked Wentworth, who started purring loudly. "He seems to have settled right in."

"He has. It's like we've always been together. He loves the—"

I stopped myself. I was about to say 'ghosts', then corrected myself. "Er, the tuna-flavoured treats."

O'Malley looked at his watch. "I'd better get going. Another early start tomorrow, trying to find this killer."

"Thanks for coming, and for the food."

I followed him to the door. But when he reached it, instead of opening it, he turned to face me. His eyes searched mine with a quiet intensity that made me catch my breath. The space between us dissolved as he moved closer, his hand brushing my arm. The outside world felt a million miles away.

Slowly, he leaned in, and I found myself mirroring his movement, our faces drawing nearer. My heart pounded, and I could feel the warmth of his breath as our lips hovered a whisper apart.

But before they could meet, a sudden gust of cold air blew through the room, and the lampshade above us swayed. In the living room, someone giggled.

Lily.

"What was that?" he asked, looking around him with a mixture of confusion and concern.

I forced a smile. "Uh, probably just a draught."

He nodded, but was clearly unsettled. "That was … weird."

"Yeah," I replied, my heart still racing for more reasons than one.

The moment was broken. I could have killed Lily.

Except that she was already dead.

"I'll see you soon." He opened the door and was gone.

I stormed into the living room. "Lily!"

Lily appeared out of thin air. "What?"

"Why did you do that?"

She giggled.

"We almost kissed and you ruined it. Now he thinks my house is haunted."

"Well, it *is* haunted."

My eyes narrowed. "Are you jealous?"

Lily laughed. "No! Although he is handsome."

"Promise me you won't do that again."

Lily shot me a look and carried on giggling.

I folded my arms. "In that case, I won't help you get the enchanted moonstone from the museum."

Lily stopped laughing.

"I mean it. You can't go disrupting my love life, or rather, lack of one. O'Malley is the first man I've met in a very long time who I like, and who likes me, too. Maybe nothing will come of it, but I need to find out on my own, without you interfering." I felt my anger rising as the words spilled out.

Lily floated in front of me, bobbing up and down a little, with an overly dramatic sad expression on her face.

"Lily." It was Lady Camilla, she floated in, too. "Trinity is correct. You must not interfere like this, moonstone or no. It is unseemly. Unladylike, even."

Lily sighed. "All right. I promise."

"Repeat after me: I promise not to interfere with Trinity and O'Malley," Lady Camilla said sternly.

Lily parroted, "I promise not to interfere with Trinity and O'Malley." She turned to me. "Will that do?"

I gave her a brief satisfied nod.

CHAPTER 26

After closing time the next day, I stayed in the town centre for the festival's grand parade of morris dancers. All the morris sides paraded down the esplanade, then went to the stage at Blackmore Gardens where there would be more dancing.

I found a spot to stand near the start. The first side was the local Sidmouth Steppers, a team of ladies in red tabards and black clogs. They danced along, leading fifteen other sides of different dancers: Cotswold, Border, North West, and even Molly dancers, dressed in a kaleidoscope of colours.

The ghosts seemed to enjoy the parade, too. Lily and Mr Wickers floated among them, laughing.

"Did they have morris dancers in your day?" I asked the others, as I watching the procession pass.

"Yes, but I never watched them," said Mr Darby, who was floating next to me. "They were for the lower classes."

I glanced at him. Despite his words, he was smiling and enjoying the parade, too.

When the last of the dancers had passed, I fell in behind them, intending to follow them to Blackmore Gardens. But then I spied Gordon's crêpe stall and my tummy growled. I joined the queue.

"Oh, hello," he said, when I got to the front. "What can I get you?"

"I'll have a crêpe with chocolate sauce, please," I replied, remembering the one I'd seen him make a few days ago.

Gordon poured batter onto the griddle.

"Did you hear about Danny Vance?" I asked, as he spread the liquid out.

Gordon looked up. "Terrible, isn't it? He needs police protection, in case whoever did it tries again." He loosened the crêpe with his palette knife. "I did see that young girl with him. You know, Jazz. They were sat in a pub."

So he'd seen them that night, too. "That's a coincidence. You saw them the night Martin was killed, as well."

Gordon looked up, his eyes searching me. Then he relaxed. "Did I not mention I saw them that night?"

"No. You said you went straight home after packing up here."

"Must have forgotten to tell you." He shrugged.

Mr Wickers flew into the crêpe tent and looked around again. "Not as messy as last time, but by the looks of that cash tin, he is making a healthy profit still. Very commendable."

My eyes fell on the tin he mentioned; this time it was open, and full of bank notes.

"So when you saw them in the pub, were you leaving for the night?"

He nodded. "Yes, yes that's right. I'd just packed up, and I was ready to enjoy the festival as much as I could. Now I'm all the way down here, I don't see a great deal." He handed me the crêpe.

"Next year will be different," I said, recalling Laura's promise.

I found a bench looking out to sea and ate my crêpe.

"What do you think of that?" I asked the ghosts, between bites. "He saw Jazz and Danny, too."

"Not much," said Lady Camilla. "It was busy. Hardly surprising that they were seen by others."

I stared out to sea. It was a calm evening, and the sea was as still as a lake. Small groups of families played on the pebbles, swimming or paddling.

"What are you thinking about?" Lady Camilla demanded. Her shrill voice cut through my thoughts.

"I'm mulling over the list of suspects. Gordon has admitted to seeing Martin and Jazz late on the night of Martin's murder as well as Danny and Jazz on the night he was attacked. And Gordon had a grudge against Martin. But I don't know of any grudge against Danny."

Mr Darby floated down. "We know all of this. But don't forget Sarah."

"Sarah?" She was the no-nonsense festival coordinator until Martin had sacked her. Yes. Of course. How could I have forgotten about her.

I needed to find out where Sarah lived, so that I could ask about her movements on the night Martin died.

I decided to take the easiest route, and asked the café and restaurant messenger group where she lived. No one knew, but someone said that Sarah had been helping out at Jurassic Loaf, one of the bakeries on the high street, which was owned by a family member.

CHAPTER 27

I nipped out of the tearoom during my break the next day and stepped inside the small bakery, and the warm, comforting aroma of freshly baked bread and sweet pastries hit me. When my eyes adjusted to the dark interior, I spotted Sarah behind the counter.

She was standing at the till, her hair in a messy ponytail. Her red tabard made me feel as though I'd stepped back into the 1980s. In fact, the whole shop felt like a throwback. She was serving an elderly lady, waiting for her to count out coins for the small paper-wrapped loaf sitting on the counter.

I hung back, examining the cakes in the glass cabinet. Flapjacks, jam doughnuts, rock cakes, Belgian buns, millionaire slices. No scones or Devon apple cake…

The elderly lady shuffled out and I stepped up. Sarah's smile remained in place as she took in my Regency gown, but it didn't quite reach her eyes.

"Good morning," she said, her tone polite but guarded. "What would you like?"

"Hi, Sarah. Do you remember me from the festival committee meeting?"

Sarah nodded. "Have you run out of scones?"

I laughed, unsure if she was joking. "I wondered if we could talk about Martin."

She put her hands on her hips. "What business is it of yours?"

She had a point. "Well, er, I'm just trying to get to the bottom of it all."

Her eyes narrowed, but through them, I could still see a cold, long stare directed straight at me.

"What about him?" she said eventually.

"You were his festival coordinator, so I was hoping you could provide some insights into his life and relationships."

Sarah gave a harsh laugh. "Insights? Oh yes, I've got plenty of those. But I doubt they're the kind you're looking for."

She was more abrasive than I had expected. "Any information could be helpful," I said.

Sarah glanced around the empty shop, then leaned in, her voice low and intense. "Martin Hawthorne was a miserable excuse for a human being, and working for him was absolute hell."

The venom in her voice made me step back. I'd expected some resentment, but the depth of her hatred surprised me.

"Er, what made working for him so difficult?" I ventured.

Sarah's eyes flashed with anger. "Where do I start? He was a perfectionist, in the worst way. Nothing was ever good enough. He'd always find something to criticise."

She took a deep breath. "That wasn't even the worst of it. Martin was a master of psychological manipulation. He'd praise you one minute and make you feel on top of the world. The next minute, he'd tear you down again."

I listened intently, trying not to act too surprised. "That sounds like a nightmare work environment. Was there a specific incident that led to the argument you had? I know he was angry because of Danny Vance but it wasn't just that was it?" I didn't know, but I thought I would fish and see.

"You're really nosey, aren't you!"

I shrugged. "I run a tearoom. People come in and gossip."

That seemed to placate her. She sighed and shook her head. "All right. I'll tell you. He didn't sack me because of Danny Vance. He was mad about it, that's for sure, but he wanted the biggest bands in the folk scene at this festival, and he told me to sort it 'at any cost'. Those were his exact words. I reminded him of them after the committee meeting."

"So why did he sack you?"

"Because I refused to falsify financial documents for him."

My jaw dropped. "That's a serious accusation."

"I know." Sarah nodded, her expression grim. "And yes, I considered reporting him. But who'd believe me over the great Martin Hawthorne?"

"Was that the first time he'd asked?"

"Yes. But it was big. I'd discovered a gap in the festival bank account of twenty thousand pounds. He said it had been used to pay one of the marquee companies in cash for a cheaper rate."

I scoffed. "Sounds suspicious."

"That's because it was. We never did anything in cash for the festival. All the books get audited."

"So what happened next?"

"Nothing. He sacked me. He said I was too difficult to work with, and that was that."

"You must have resented him for putting you in a difficult position."

"Resent him?" Sarah scoffed. "I hated him. And you know what? I'm not sorry he's dead. The world's a better place without him."

I was taken aback by Sarah's bluntness. It was refreshing, but deeply concerning. She had a clear motive for murder.

"Does Laura know?"

"Laura? Yeah, she knows. I told her everything the day Martin was found dead. But she took Martin's side. Said he was trustworthy and the money would have gone to the company. I should have known. She was his golden girl. Wouldn't be surprised if they were having an affair."

She folded her arms. "So I suppose now you think *I* killed him."

I held up a hand. "I'm not accusing you of anything, Sarah." Although, I was thinking it.

Sarah stared at me, her expression a mixture of anger and incredulity. Then she burst out laughing. It wasn't a pleasant sound: there was something in the laughter which set me on edge.

"Oh, this is rich," she said, wiping her eyes. "You think I murdered Martin! I wish I could take the credit for ridding the world of that bastard, but unfortunately, I can't."

"What do you mean?"

"I mean, that as much as I hated Martin, I didn't kill him. I have an alibi."

"Care to share it with me?"

Sarah smirked. "I was with my sister. She'd gone into labour and I was with her. I went straight to the maternity ward at Honiton Hospital, and I was with her the entire night." Her smirk broadened. "You can check with the hospital staff. No one can pin Martin's murder on me."

Well, that was an unexpected turn of events. I puzzled over how I could check her alibi. The maternity ward at Honiton Hospital was small. I was sure Aunt Ruby might know some of the staff there, too. Honiton was a only few miles away.

"Well, thank you for your time, Sarah."

She nodded, her bitterness gone. "I meant what I said about Martin. He was a terrible person who hurt a lot of people. Whoever killed him... Well, let's just say they did the world a favour."

Her words made me feel uncomfortable. No one else had described this side of Martin. It wasn't that I didn't believe

Sarah, but Laura, who had also worked closely with Martin, hadn't mentioned anything like this. "Murder is never the answer, regardless of the victim's character."

"Maybe not," she said. "But sometimes karma catches up with people in unexpected ways."

I turned to leave. As I reached the door, Sarah said, "If I was investigating the murder, I'd check out Ethan Cole, Martin's business partner. If anyone had a reason to want Martin dead, it was him."

I faced her. "Why is that?"

"Martin wasn't above stabbing a friend in the back if it benefited him. Ethan found that out the hard way."

I left the bakery, my mind buzzing.

My next task was to look into Ethan Cole. If Sarah was to be believed – and that was a big *if* – this case might be far more complex than it had appeared at first.

One thing was certain: Martin had made a lot of enemies. The challenge now was to figure out which one had finally snapped and decided to kill him.

I was halfway to the tearoom when I realised the ghosts had been remarkably quiet and well-behaved. In fact, they had been absent. I glanced about me – no one was near – then pressed the turquoise stone on my ring to summon them.

CHAPTER 28

The ghosts materialised one by one in front of me.

"Where were you?" I asked. "I thought you'd want to have a good look around the bakery."

Lily shuddered. "Ugh, no! There was a horrible ghost in there."

"Really? I didn't see it." My eyes narrowed. "Are you and Mr Wickers tricking me again?"

Mr Wickers floated in front of me with an innocent expression. "Not at all. The ghost was, well, rather grumpy. He was pacing back and forth, muttering about maggots in the flour and recipes that had gone wrong, and—"

"He was a crotchety old baker," said Lady Camilla. "I, for one, do *not* wish to converse with such a man."

"Why couldn't I see him, then?" I asked.

"He was in the back with the bread ovens," said Lily. "I would not return to that bakery."

"I don't intend to. What I do need to do is speak to Aunt Ruby again. First, to find out if she knows anyone who works at Honiton Hospital, then to see if she knows anything about Ethan Cole." The latter was a long shot, but I thought it was worth asking. You just never knew with Aunt Ruby.

When I got home, I video-called Aunt Ruby's number, which she answered after a few rings. This time, she wasn't on the beach. She was in a busy bar, wearing lots of make-up, and she held up a cocktail glass and grinned. "Hello, Trin, darling. How are things?"

"Hi, Aunt Ruby. Wow, you look lovely and tanned. How is the holiday?"

"Splendid, darling, splendid! Is it still all kicking off in Sidmouth?"

"You could say that."

"Have they found the killer? Or rather, have *you* found the killer?"

I chuckled. "Not yet, but not from lack of trying. Look, do you know anything about a man called Ethan Cole?"

"Who? Never heard of him. Ethan, you say?" She turned to her left, which was presumably where her friend was. "Sheila, have you heard of Ethan Cole?"

"Ethan who?" said Sheila. "Cole? No, I don't think so."

"Give me some context, Trin."

"He's a business associate of Martin's."

"He's a business associate of Martin's," Aunt Ruby repeated loudly. I wondered how many of those cocktails she'd had.

"No, not heard of him," Sheila bellowed. "Martin never mentioned him."

"Oh well, thanks anyway. Oh, and what do you know about Sarah? The festival coordinator?"

"Well, now, I do know about her," said Aunt Ruby, looking very knowing.

"Go on, then, tell me what you know."

"She likes a drink, if you know what I mean." Aunt Ruby set down her own cocktail glass with a loud clink and mimed someone drinking from a bottle.

"Oh, I see. Do you know why she and Martin didn't get on?"

"Not a clue. Why? Is she one of your suspects?"

"Yes. When I spoke to her about Martin's death, she was over the moon that he'd been killed. She didn't even try to hide it."

"Alibi?"

"That's the thing, she has one. She says that on the night of Martin's murder she was with her sister in the maternity ward in Honiton Hospital. Do you know anyone who works there?"

"Hmm. I think Helen Hillingsworth is still there."

"Have you got her phone number or email?"

"Oh, Trin, I'm on *holiday*. She's a friend of mine on social media, so you can just message her there."

"But I don't know her. It feels a bit strange to—"

"Ooh, look over there…" Aunt Ruby turned her phone and showed me two bronzed young men with crisp white shirts and slicked-back hair.

"Yes, very handsome. Are you sure you don't have Helen's—"

"Come on, Sheila. Let's see if we can make them squirm."

I sighed; there was no hope for her. "Bye, Aunt Ruby."

She wasn't listening. I ended the call.

Lady Camilla huffed. "Disgusting behaviour."

I shrugged. "There's not much I can do about it."

"You must have a severe word with your aunt when she returns. That is no way for a lady to act."

I shrugged. "She won't listen to me."

"Then put the ring on her finger and I'll speak to her."

I chuckled. "Not likely! Is that even allowed?"

Mr Collingwood floated up to me. "There are no rules as to who can wear the ring."

"Have past ring-holders allowed their friends to wear the ring, then?" I hadn't considered letting anyone else wear the ring, let alone giving it to them to put on. I touched the ring, feeling a sudden possessiveness of it. What if I gave the ring to someone else and they wouldn't give it back? What if the ghosts preferred that person? What if it made the person go mad? I could imagine that happening.

Then I imagined myself giving the ring to O'Malley. What would he think of it? It would certainly make things easier if I could talk to him about the one thing I couldn't mention to anyone else ... then I shook my head. This wasn't *The Lord of the Rings*. For now, it was best for me to keep it to myself.

"One or two past ring-owners have allowed others to wear the ring," said Mr Collingwood, reverently, "but I would advise against it."

"You know what; I think you're right."

That night, I opened my decrepit laptop and looked for Aunt Ruby's social media profile. Helen was listed as a connection. I clicked the message button and started typing.

Hi Helen, I'm Ruby Bishop's niece. I run the Regency tearoom in Sidmouth. I wondered if you could verify whether Sarah—

How ridiculous this was. Would I really send a message to a healthcare worker, asking them to verify someone's alibi? I wasn't the police. And anyway, wasn't all that confidential information?

I deleted the message. I'd find another way. Maybe I could confirm it somehow through Sarah's sister. I reopened the laptop and found Sarah's profile, then her sister's. She had posted an album of photos a few days ago. She was sitting up in a hospital bed, holding a tiny baby, and next to her was Sarah. That didn't prove Sarah was with her at the time of the murder, though. I'd have to try another way.

Now for Ethan Cole.

I searched for his name and found him easily. He was a frequent visitor to Sidmouth, perhaps to visit Martin, his business partner.

Then I hit a problem. His status said that he'd moved to the United Arab Emirates six months ago, and the photos he'd posted bore that out. From his business profile, he was some kind of influencer. And he was very different to Martin. Younger, for a start.

All his photos showed selfies of him in posh restaurants or enjoying gourmet food. Some showed him looking out over Dubai. His other posts urged people to join him on livestreams, or to direct-message him for business coaching.

I turned to the ghosts, who were floating around me, watching. "Whatever Ethan Cole's relationship with Martin, it doesn't look as if he's left Dubai recently. He posted a photo showing Dubai on the day of Martin's murder, as well as the day before and after. I know you can schedule social media posts, but it doesn't look as if he's been back here for months."

Mr Darby moved closer. "Have you considered that Martin's murderer and the person who attacked Danny could be two different people?"

I considered this. "You could be right. The person who attacked Danny could be copying the attack on Martin to confuse us. Or the attacks could be completely unrelated."

"I doubt that they are unrelated," said Mr Darby. "After all, the two men were in a popular music group." I glimpsed the ghost of a smile.

Wentworth walked in and jumped on the chair next to me, purring and rubbing my arm with his head.

"Hello, there." I stroked him. "Looking for some love?"

He put a paw on the keyboard and I laughed. "Not very subtle." I closed the laptop and let him move onto my lap.

Wentworth didn't sit down, though. He stood there, receiving all the attention I could give him, until Mr Wickers appeared. "Let's see if this works." He recited a short incantation, and a small, glowing orb appeared.

"Wow, that's impressive," I said.

Mr Wickers gave me a satisfied smile and made a gesture. The orb danced in front of Wentworth, then shot to the other side of the room. Wentworth jumped down and chased the orb, but as soon as he got close, it jerked away.

I laughed. "Oh, Wentworth, that is super cute."

After a minute, the cat flopped on the floor, his head moving as he watched the orb. It came closer and he ducked his head, eyes wide.

"You need to let him catch it at least once," said Lily. "Otherwise, he'll get bored."

Mr Wickers moved his hand and the orb hovered by Wentworth's paw. He tried to trap the orb but his paw passed right through it.

"Well, I guess that's close enough," I said. "We're both chasing something, aren't we?" I murmured.

The ghosts exchanged glances but said nothing. I turned back to my laptop, determined to figure out what I was missing.

CHAPTER 29

As I walked to the tearoom the next morning, I passed the town noticeboard. I glanced at it, then stopped as my mind processed the notices stuck on it. One said, *New Health Visitor Drop-In Sessions: weighing and advice available.* I remembered going to a similar event in London when Oliver was tiny. A health visitor would be there, and you could weigh your baby, get general advice, and meet other new mothers. I'd stayed friends with some of the women I'd met there, for a long time, only drifting apart when our children went to different schools or they moved away. The drop-in was in the library at two o'clock. I decided to pop in and see if Sarah's sister was there.

At just after two, I made my excuses to Emma, Carole, and Alan and set off for the library. It was a long shot, I knew: not all new mothers attended drop-ins. She might have trouble getting there, and the town was busy with the festival. But I had to try.

When I went inside, the library was quiet except for the children's section, where a group of women with prams had congregated near a health visitor with some weigh scales. I approached and quickly identified Beth, who was chatting to another mother, her baby in a pram.

She looked tired, but despite having given birth just the week before, she looked remarkably well-groomed. I'd never looked that neat and tidy after giving birth. Dealing with a tiny human had been a shock, and I'd experienced a severe lack of sleep.

Mr Wickers floated near me, rubbing his chin. "How will you approach her?"

"I'll coo over her baby," I whispered.

"You must hurry, then. She seems about to leave."

Beth said goodbye to the woman she'd been talking to, then wheeled her pram towards the door.

I made my move, intercepting her by the history section. "Oh, what a beautiful baby!" I cooed. "How old is your little one?"

Beth smiled and looked me up and down in my Regency costume. "Thank you! He's just a week old. It's been a whirl-wind, but I'm getting the hang of it."

"I remember it well! I have a boy too: he's this high now." I indicated high above my head. "I'm Trinity, by the way: I run the Regency tearoom. You must have had a busy time recently. Did you get much help from family or friends?"

"Oh yes, my family have been brilliant."

That was very nice, but not the information I needed. "How was your labour? Did you have him at home or in the hospital?"

Beth shrugged. "I wanted to have him at home, but in the end I decided to go into hospital. My sister stayed with me the whole time. She didn't leave my side until this little one made his appearance."

"Wow! I wish I'd had a sister to stay with me when I gave birth. My husband was hopeless: you know what men are like. So, you're close to your sister, then?"

"Yes. I don't know how I would have managed without her."

So that was that. We fell silent as we gazed at the baby, who really was gorgeous.

"Well, I'd better let you get on," I said. "Thanks for the chat."

"Bye, then." She pushed the pram towards the door.

"That was easy," said Mr Wickers, as the door closed behind her.

"It was," said Mr Darby. "Though all this talk of childbirth is not appropriate for a gentleman to hear." He scowled and floated off.

My business at the library complete, I wandered through Blackmore Gardens, past the church and the town square, heading for the tearoom.

When there was hardly anyone else around, I spoke to the ghosts. "Sarah and Danny both have an alibi, Laura and Jazz have no real motive, and Ethan Cole wasn't even in the country. That leaves Martin's girlfriends."

"Don't forget Gordon," said Lily. "He has a motive, and no alibi."

"Gordon?" I stared at her. No one kills for a street food pitch – that's ridiculous! I think I should talk to Danny again. Maybe now his head has cleared, he'll remember something about the attack."

———

I couldn't remember which caravan was Danny's, so I let the ghosts lead the way. I was rather anxious, as I wasn't sure what to say. As far as I could work out, there were three reasons for what had happened to Danny. Someone wanted both band members dead, Danny's attack was for a different reason from Martin's, or it was a ruse by Danny to divert suspicion about Martin's murder.

I paused outside the caravan door. Music was playing softly inside.

"Ooh," said Mr Wickers, as I knocked.

The music stopped, and the door opened to reveal Jazz, dressed in ripped jeans and a pink T-shirt. My heart sank.

"Who is it?" said Danny, from inside.

She turned her head. "The tearoom lady."

That was new. "Can I come in?"

"Yeah, let her in," said Danny.

Jazz opened the door wider and I stepped inside. Danny was sitting on the settee, holding a guitar, a large dressing still on his head. "Don't be shy," he said, grinning.

"It's not what it looks like," Jazz said, immediately. She sat on the settee and I sat opposite them.

Danny chuckled. "Yeah. She's young enough to be my daughter."

"You wouldn't be the first or the last pop star to have a much younger girlfriend," I said, as casually as I could.

"I prefer a more mature woman." Danny winked at me. "Anyway, I'm taken. My girlfriend's out shopping in Exeter. After all the kerfuffle, she needs retail therapy. It's nice to see you again, though, Trinity. Can't stay away from me, can you? Nice to have a groupie, after all this time."

"Groupie?" I gasped. "As much as I liked your music back in the day, I'm not that type of woman."

Danny put the guitar beside him. "So, to what do I owe the pleasure?"

"I wondered if you'd remembered anything from the night you were attacked."

"Sadly not. Now then, Trinity, I can see you giving me the side-eye and there's no need. I know it's strange that a man my age would mentor a young girl like Jazz, but she dropped a bombshell the other day." He glanced at Jazz, who was sitting quietly in the corner of the settee. "Go on, Jazz, tell her."

She gazed up at me. "My dad was the third member of Velvet Vortex."

"There was a third member?" I thought back to the pop magazines and TV shows of my childhood. I could only remember two members: Martin and Danny.

She nodded. "He left a few months before the group became famous."

"Yeah," said Danny. "Johnno was with us to start with, but his parents moved to Australia and he went, too."

"You don't sound Australian," I said to Jazz.

"He moved back to the UK a few years later and married my mum. He had a few solo singles, but they never topped the charts. Not like Velvet Vortex."

"Johnno wrote some of our biggest hits. And don't worry – he got the songwriting credit and the money. Which now goes to Jazz here."

"Where is he now?"

Jazz looked down. "He passed away three years ago."

"Oh. I'm sorry."

"He never really got over his demons," she said, sadly. "It was the drink that finished him, in the end."

"And now you've come to Sidmouth, to touch base with the other band members?"

Jazz nodded. "That's what Martin and I were talking about on the night he died. I told him who I was, and that I wanted to know more about my dad from back then. My father never really talked about those days. But I know he regretted moving to Australia and missing it all."

Danny smiled. "I was just telling Jazz about the time all three of us gatecrashed a party in Chelsea, trying to meet some posh supermodel. She thought we'd come to trash the joint, but we just wanted some booze and a boogie. Happy days." He shook his head. "It was such a shame that Johnno left the band: he was the glue that held us together. If me and Martin argued, he'd make us see sense. And if he'd stuck around, maybe we'd have stayed together for longer, and not been at war all these years."

Lady Camilla, who had been listening intently, sniffed. "Well, that is a revelation."

"Why *did* you fall out with Martin?" I asked.

Danny's face darkened. "I was never in with Martin. We were never friends. We were both mates with Jazz's father, Johnno, but separately. Chalk and cheese, Martin and me were. We were on the verge of splitting up when we had our first top ten hit, you know. That kept us together, because no one was going to walk away from that. In the end, we drifted apart. There wasn't any one argument that finished things: it all accumulated till we couldn't face going on."

"So you really have no idea who might want to attack you both?" I asked.

"Nah. Could be a crazed fan from back then, I guess. Someone who couldn't let go. But honestly, I don't think it was. They'd care a lot more than Martin and I ever did, for one thing. And it wasn't young Jazz. She's been in here chatting with me a couple of hours. She could have finished me off easy in that time, if she wanted." He chuckled, and Jazz managed a half smile.

Looking at the pair of them, I actually believed Jazz now. I didn't think she'd attacked Danny. Or Martin either.

CHAPTER 30

made my way home, my mind churning with this new information. Jazz was not the murderer, and it seemed that Danny wasn't either. So who could it be?

As I passed the Radway Inn, I heard live folk music playing and paused by the door to listen. They were playing a traditional tune, and I could hear fiddles, a drum, and a flute. I knew there were lots of sessions in pubs and other venues throughout the festival week, as well as the formal gigs, but I'd never attended one in a pub.

Mr Wickers and Lily floated through the wall, then came out a moment later. "It's an Irish music session," said Lily. "You should go in. It's even more delightful when you're inside." She giggled.

The music drew me in, and I entered the pub. It was small: the bar was almost immediately in front of me. To the left, six or seven musicians were seated around a table, playing their hearts out. It was a lively, upbeat tune, and I felt myself relax instantly.

I ordered a G and T at the bar. "Why don't you move over there?" said Lily. "There's room at a table." She pointed and giggled, and then I spotted him.

DI Cormac O'Malley.

He was sitting at a small table near the back: quieter, but still within earshot of the music. In front of him was a half-drunk pint of Guinness.

He must have sensed me, because he looked up. Our eyes met, and we smiled at each other.

"Go and join him," Lily said, in my ear.

I didn't need any persuasion.

He stood up when I reached the table. "Care to join me?" he asked, and pointed to the space beside him.

"If you don't mind."

"Not at all."

I put my glass on the table and we sat down.

"I don't suppose it's a coincidence that you're here when there's an Irish folk session going on."

He chuckled. "Not at all. I saw it advertised and decided to come. I don't usually get homesick, but it's nice to have a little reminder of home now and again."

I sipped my G and T. "Do you play an instrument?"

"No, never learnt. You?"

"Piano, when I was little. I hated it and begged my mother to let me stop, which she did. Now, of course, I regret it. I could have been a great proficient by now if I'd learnt."

I studied O'Malley's face to see if he recognised my reworking of Lady Catherine de Bourgh's words from *Pride and Prejudice,* but he just nodded. I didn't try to look for Lady Camilla. She would either be somewhere in the pub or just outside.

I took another sip of my drink. "I was on my way back from visiting Danny Vance, actually."

"Really? Out of the kindness of your heart? More scones? Or to try and find more information?"

I smiled. "Jazz was there. Did you know she's the daughter of the third original band member from Velvet Vortex?"

O'Malley took a sip of his Guinness. "I did know that, yes."

Always one step ahead. But if he'd share more about the case with me, it would save me a lot of time.

"Did you speak to Sarah, too?" I asked.

"I have."

"Still no arrest, then?"

He looked into his pint. "Not yet. Some might say I shouldn't be sat here with a pint, but out looking for the murderer."

"Everyone needs time off."

"True. And getting to the pub helps clear my head."

"It's a puzzling case. Every time I think I've spotted a motive, the person turns out to have an alibi."

He sat back. "Alibis can be faked, you know."

"I'm sure you've checked all that."

"With cases like these, there are always lots of uncertainties. I've found it's best to let things come to their natural conclusion." He picked up his glass and took a draught. When he put it down, he seemed to be debating something in his head.

"My grandmother used to tell me stories about the sidhe," he said, eventually, his voice low. "Old Irish spirits, the guardians of the land. She believed that those who truly understood the ways of the earth could ask for their help when in great need."

He locked his hypnotic eyes on mine, a faint smile on his lips.

"I've never heard of the sidhe," I said, feeling rather confused.

"They're part of Irish mythology, like fairies or spirits, connected to the natural world. They are said to live in mounds or hills, and they inhabit an invisible parallel world that sometimes interacts with ours."

"Oh. I see," I said, though I wasn't sure I did.

"My grandmother also used to say that certain people were born with a touch of the *céad draíocht*. The first magic. Not witchcraft: nothing like that. More a sense of knowing things without being told. She called it 'the gift'."

I swallowed. "And do you think you have that?" I said it in a half-joking way, but I was genuinely curious.

He just smiled again but didn't reply.

"Are they good or bad?" I frowned, frustrated at his silence.

"A little bit of both."

The music stopped, and the thread was broken.

He sat back and sighed. "I need to get back soon – I have the kids tomorrow. Can I walk you home?"

I could walk home perfectly well on my own, but I didn't want us to part company just yet. "Sure."

When we left the pub, our conversation flowed again, and we reached my house far too quickly.

"Thank you for the company, and for walking me back," I said.

He smiled. "Any time. But be warned: I charge double for a round trip."

Out of the corner of my eye I saw the ghosts disappearing into my house, though Lily had to be dragged by Lady Camilla.

We were alone.

O'Malley looked into my eyes again, I leaned in slightly, and he did, too…

My neighbour's front door opened and Mrs Bailey stepped out. Yet again, the spell was broken.

He looked down and bit his lip. "Well, goodnight."

"Goodnight," I said, reluctantly, and took out my key.

I watched him walk away.

His story about the sidhe and "the gift" tugged at something I couldn't quite put my finger on. Was it just a family story, or did he truly believe in it?

I sighed and glanced toward Mrs Bailey, who was now putting the bins out, oblivious to what she'd interrupted. Typical.

CHAPTER 31

When I got inside the house, the ghosts were waiting for me.

"Thanks for leaving O'Malley and me alone," I said. "I do appreciate it. However, Mrs Bailey interrupted us."

Mr Collingwood bowed. "We are not interested in that."

"I was!" Lily giggled.

Mr Collingwood cleared his throat. "We have been discussing the case and all the suspects."

"And?"

"You said that Gordon did not have an alibi."

"No, but his motive is flaky. I just can't see anyone killing over a street food stall."

Mr Collingwood bowed and opened his mouth to speak again, but Lady Camilla got in first. "*We* want to investigate him."

"What do you mean?"

"All you will have to do is go near his house. We will enter and look through his belongings for anything suspicious."

I thought about it for a moment. It seemed like a good

idea, although what they would find that linked him to the murder, I wasn't sure.

"He must live nearby. It won't take you long to get there."

I flopped on the sofa. "I'm tired, though. I need some sleep. Seriously? You want me to go out again?" I looked at the clock on the wall opposite. It was quarter past eleven.

"You will not have time in the morning," said Lady Camilla. "As you will open the tearoom early." She stared me down. I could tell she wouldn't take no for an answer.

I sighed. "All right. But I think you're wrong. I'll do it, but only because I can say 'I told you so' when you find nothing."

I looked up Gordon's address on the Companies House website and found that he lived in Sidford, just north of Sidmouth. I drove to his house and parked a short distance away. The ghosts floated off down the path, and I stayed in the car.

Lily returned first. "We haven't found anything yet."

"Is Gordon in?" I imagined him sitting in an armchair, perhaps watching television, while the ghosts swooped around him and discussed their findings.

"No, he isn't. But there are lots of papers and other things. He seems to be a hoarder. It's taking us a while to go through it all." She floated off again.

It seemed to take the ghosts an extraordinarily long time to search Gordon's house, though perhaps that was because I was sitting on my own in a dark, silent car, with the engine off, trying not to attract attention.

Lily returned again and reported that they still hadn't found anything. Meanwhile, I had to try and look inconspicuous when a man walking a dog strolled past. I took out my phone and pretended I was making a call.

Eventually, the ghosts came floating back, at a speed that suggested they had something to tell me.

"We've found it!" cried Lily.

"Found what?"

Mr Wickers spoke. "There was a safe. Of course, it presented no barrier to us. We found a collection of documents, including a small notebook, and a huge stash of bank notes arranged in bundles. I counted twelve thousand pounds."

I goggled at him. "Twelve grand? That's an obscene amount of money."

Mr Wickers gave me a satisfied nod.

"But that still doesn't mean he killed Martin."

"Now then." He wagged a finger. "In the small notebook was a page *Martin Hawthorne* and a list of dates with different amounts."

"Okay. Did it say what the money was for?"

"No."

I thought for a moment. "What other names are in the book?"

"There are several. But it seems those people pay money to Gordon."

"Could he be running some sort of illegal gambling ring?"

"Perhaps," said Mr Wickers, "but I think it more likely that he is a moneylender."

"A moneylender? I'm not sure about that."

Lady Camilla sniffed. "It doesn't matter if you're sure or not. You must follow the evidence."

She was right. "Okay, so if Gordon is an illegal moneylender, why would he be paying Martin?"

"Maybe Martin had invested capital in the scheme?" said Lily. "Gordon could be paying him back."

"It's possible. But why would he kill Martin?" I drummed my fingers on the steering wheel.

"Perhaps Martin didn't want to be Gordon's partner any more," said Mr Wickers. "Maybe he wanted to branch out on his own."

"Or Martin could have been blackmailing Gordon," I said.

"Either way, this shows a clear link between Martin and Gordon, other than their fight over the crêpe pitch."

"Shush!" exclaimed Mr Darby.

"What is it?" I whispered.

"Gordon has arrived. He is pulling up in his car."

True enough, I saw car headlights in the side mirror and ducked. A car pulled around mine and turned into the drive.

"Tell me when he's gone inside," I said. "Then I can start the car and go."

"No!" said Mr Darby. "Wait here, so that we can see what he does."

"All right, but I'm not staying here all night."

The ghosts floated back to the house. After a minute, I tentatively sat up. Hiding in a car wasn't at all comfortable.

Eventually, Lily returned. "He checked the ledger, and he's just picked up his car keys again. Duck down: he's going to leave."

I did as she said. Sure enough, I heard a car door slam and an engine start. Above me, the car's rear lights came on.

I waited for Gordon to leave, then sat up and started my car. "I'll follow him."

Mr Wickers clapped his hands. "Oh, goody! A car chase!"

CHAPTER 32

Following a car in the dark at a safe distance wasn't easy, and I couldn't help thinking that I might be doing the wrong thing. What if Gordon realised I was following him and took me on a wild-goose chase? What if he was just visiting a friend or relative and it was all perfectly innocent? In the end, I put it out of my mind and concentrated on following him.

Gordon drove to Sidmouth, to the car park next to the Ham, and the main festival area. It was half-gone midnight now, and the place was dead. The last gig would have finished some time ago, and the crowds dispersed. I pulled up a good distance away so that I could watch his next move. He got out of his car and walked to the main marquee. I didn't hesitate. I got out of the car and followed. I was just in time to see Gordon disappear behind the ticket booth. The exact same spot where I'd found Martin dead.

The ghosts floated ahead and disappeared behind the booth, too.

I lurked in the shadows of a nearby food tent. Two people appeared and also went behind the booth.

Lily floated back to me. "They're talking to Gordon, and giving him money."

"Do you know who they are?"

"No, but they handed over a lot of cash."

"So it could be illegal moneylending."

Lily pursed her lips. "It looks that way."

A minute or so later, the two people walked off towards the town. The other ghosts emerged and came over to me.

"How much did they give him?" I asked.

"A great deal of money," said Mr Darby. "From what they said, those men have been collecting cash on Gordon's behalf."

"It must be a big racket, then."

"Indubitably," said Mr Darby.

"I must tell O'Malley." I strode in the opposite direction to the ticket booth but my foot caught a tent rope and I fell flat on my face. "Ow!"

"Uh-oh," said Mr Wickers.

As I was scrambling to get up, Gordon came out from behind the booth. "You!"

I stood up and brushed myself down.

"Now, what are you doing here at this time of night, Trinity? More snooping?" Instead of the open, happy Gordon I'd talked to before, his manner had changed to threatening.

Well, he wasn't wrong. "You killed Martin," I said, facing him square-on. "Not because of the pitch, but because you were in some sort of money-lending scam together."

"Very good. You've been doing your homework, haven't you?"

"So what happened? Did you fall out? Or did Martin find out you were up to something he didn't know about?"

"He borrowed from me and had problems paying me back. The same old story. Then he threatened to expose me, so I had to deal with him."

"But why Danny?"

Gordon's expression had a note of regret. "To deflect suspicion, by making it look as if someone wanted both band members dead."

I could feel my blood pressure rising. "That's a horrible thing to do to someone."

"I wasn't going to kill him! I'm not heartless! I had to kill Martin. I had good reason."

"It's heartless to kill anyone," I found myself saying.

"Yes, well, if you'd kept your nose out of all this, you wouldn't be my next victim."

I stood as tall as I could, though I was quaking inside. "I have no intention of being your next victim, so you might as well go to the police station and confess. O'Malley's on your case, you know." I gazed around me. Where were the ghosts?

"*Move.*" Gordon grabbed me and pushed me into the marquee. No one would see what he was doing. And who would be wandering around the festival site at this time of night? I shivered. Where had the ghosts got to? As Gordon lumbered into the tent, I felt for the ring on my finger and pressed the stone in the middle to summon them.

Lily floated through the side of the tent. "We're still here," she said, "and we have a plan."

I backed away from Gordon and realised I was on the stage. It was higher than it looked, from an audience perspective, but I could jump down and run to another exit. If it wasn't secured…

A moment later, smoke began to curl slowly towards me from the front of the stage. The ghosts were all standing by the smoke machines, which were now on full output.

I frowned. "How…?"

Gordon moved towards me, flailing his arms to try and clear the smoke. "What do you mean, how? And why are the smoke machine on?"

Mr Collingwood bowed. "I managed to persuade the

smoke machines to switch themselves on to maximum capacity."

Smoke billowed towards us. "Run into the smoke and we'll guide you," called Mr Collingwood.

I ran into the white clouds. It was confusing, and my eyes stung, but Lily's form glowed faintly, an ethereal light in the haze, her translucent hand outstretched towards me. Her smile was calm, reassuring, and she gestured urgently, beckoning me to follow.

"This way!" she called, her voice cutting clearly through the confusion, as if it came from inside my head rather than around me. Her movements were quick and decisive, weaving through the smoke with ease. I followed her, trusting her implicitly, focusing only on the soft shimmer of her figure ahead of me.

I could hear Gordon close behind, though, and felt a rush of air as he tried to grab me. I moved faster, but his fingers closed around my arm and jerked me backwards.

"Get off me!" I cried, and tried to wriggle free, but he was too strong.

He laughed and grabbed my other arm, but suddenly Mr Darby's face was between Gordon and me. He looked different than normal, though. As if he were made of smoke.

"Agghhh!" Gordon let go of me. "What the heck is that?" He staggered backwards and fell on the floor.

Mr Darby swooped into Gordon's face, and he whimpered, "What the—"

The ghosts took it in turns to swoop at him. "You evil man!" cried Lady Camilla, as she bore down on him, at least twice her usual size. Gordon screamed as the ghosts attacked again and again, his eyes wide and staring.

That was the distraction I needed. Guided by Lily, I made my way to the backstage exit, out into the open, and then ran towards town as fast as I could.

The ghosts followed me, and once I was close to the high

street, I felt safe enough to stop and call O'Malley. As I listened to the phone ring, the rest of the ghosts floated over to me, looking very pleased with themselves.

He answered after a few rings: "Trinity?"

"Gordon's the murderer," I panted. "And he just tried to kill me."

"What? Where are you?"

"On the high street, by the fish restaurant."

"Wait there – I'm in the police station."

"What?"

"I never went home."

I waited, terrified Gordon would appear, and jumping at every noise I heard, even though the ghosts were keeping watch.

Two minutes later, a car pulled up, and O'Malley stepped out, his expression a mix of worry and determination. "Are you okay? Did he hurt you?"

Before I could answer, he closed the distance between us and pulled me into his arms, holding me tightly as though he needed to feel for himself that I was safe. His warmth enveloped me, and for a moment, the world faded away.

He pulled back slightly, just enough to look into my eyes, his gaze searching mine with an intensity that made my heart skip. "Tell me you're okay," he said with emotion.

"I'm fine physically, but I'm a bit shaken, that's all."

"I've called for backup, and they'll be here in a minute. Stay here. I'm going to find him."

I took hold of his arm. "Do you have to? You'll find him eventually."

"I need to go. I can handle him. Where did you last see him?"

"He was on the stage in the main marquee when I ran."

"I'll start there."

O'Malley turned and ran towards the festival area.

I stood watching him for a moment. Then I gave the

ghosts an anguished look. Lady Camilla nodded at me. "We can help guide you."

I started to run behind O'Malley, although he was fast, and I struggled to keep up.

Lily flew ahead of me, glowing faintly in the dark. "Hurry! He's already near the marquee. Gordon hasn't left yet, but you must stay back when it gets dangerous."

I ignored her warning. I couldn't just wait around. O'Malley might need me. It would be harder for Gordon to kill two people.

By the time I reached the marquee, I couldn't see O'Malley, but I could hear muffled shouting from inside the marquee.

I paused for a moment outside the side entrance I'd escaped from a few minutes before, then took a deep breath and slipped inside.

Smoke still hung in the air, making it difficult to see, but the machines were no longer on, so it was starting to clear. I could make out the faint silhouettes of O'Malley and Gordon in front of me.

Gordon held a lighting pole from the stage setup and swung it wildly, shouting incoherently. O'Malley circled him, his movements unnervingly calm, as though he were sizing up not just a man, but an animal about to strike.

"I told you to stay back!" Gordon bellowed, the pole glinting in the dim light.

O'Malley's voice, low and steady, cut through the tension. "There's nowhere left to run, Gordon. Put the pole down before you do something you'll regret even more."

The calm in his tone was unnatural, almost hypnotic, and for a moment, I could swear the air around him seemed to have a warm glow. The remaining smoke swirled toward O'Malley in unnatural patterns, almost like it was bending to his will.

Lady Camilla next to me whispered, "DI O'Malley seems to have an unusual effect on the smoke in the room."

Gordon froze. His grip on the pole faltering. "Stay back!" he barked again, but the strength in his voice wavered.

O'Malley stepped closer, his gaze locking on to Gordon's. "You're done, Gordon. There's no escape. Put it down."

For a moment, it seemed to work. Gordon lowered the pole a little, his eyes darting wildly as if he was no longer sure what was real. But then, with a roar of defiance, he swung, narrowly missing O'Malley, who dodged it.

I gasped. I wanted to help but what could I do? "Can you do something?" I whispered to the ghosts.

Mr Wickers floated close to Gordon and O'Malley. "I say leave them to it. It seems O'Malley has excellent skills in combat. Do you agree, Darby?"

Mr Darby had been watching nearby. He had his hand to his chin, assessing the situation. "Yes. Sometimes you need to leave the men to fight it out. O'Malley is younger and more agile, and he will have had training. I'd wager he has every chance of winning."

I couldn't believe it.

I didn't want their opinion; I wanted action.

But before I could protest, O'Malley sidestepped another wild swing before lunging forward. He grabbed Gordon's wrist, twisting it with precision. The pole clattered to the ground. Gordon grunted, then stumbled, caught completely off guard. O'Malley swept his legs out from under him in one fluid motion, and pinned him to the stage floor.

"Told you so!" Mr Wickers proudly exclaimed.

For a moment, O'Malley leaned close to Gordon, his voice low and almost otherworldly. "It's over." The last remnants of the smoke around them seemed to settle, as if responding to O'Malley's command.

Gordon stopped struggling, and O'Malley pulled out some handcuffs from his jacket pocket.

He turned him over, and as Gordon lay facedown on the floor, O'Malley put the cuffs on him.

The tension in my chest eased.

"All's well that ends well," Mr Darby stated.

"I'll talk to you two later," I said under my breath.

O'Malley walked towards me, holding on to Gordon, his gaze softening slightly when he saw me.

"You shouldn't have come," he said, his voice both chastising and gentle.

"I couldn't just wait." I heard a tremble in my voice. "Are you… Are you okay? He didn't hit you, did he?"

"No, I'm fine. And he won't hurt anyone else. Don't worry. I've dealt with worse … though usually not while dodging stage props."

CHAPTER 33

An hour later I was sitting in one of the interview rooms in the police station, nursing a cup of sweet tea, watched over by my cousin Francis and the ghosts.

The police backup had arrived not long after O'Malley had apprehended Gordon, and I'd come along to give my statement in the same room as last time.

O'Malley entered the room. His stubble was darker than ever, and there were shadows under his eyes. "How are you, Trinity?" He nodded to Francis, who stood up and left.

"Better now."

He sat down opposite me.

"Is Gordon all right?" I asked.

O'Malley chuckled. "The man tried to kill you, and here you are asking after him."

I had to laugh at the irony.

"He's fine, but he's muttering about ghosts. He says he saw terrible things in that marquee and that you're a witch."

I raised my eyebrows.

"I know," said O'Malley, and grinned. "This isn't the first time someone's accused you of witchcraft, is it?"

I tried to look innocent. "I can't think why."

He leaned forward a little. "Did you see any ghosts in the marquee?"

I heard Lily giggle.

I didn't want to lie to O'Malley, but I couldn't tell him the truth. "There was lots of smoke on the stage," I said. "Maybe Gordon thought he saw things." I still wanted to know how the ghosts had made themselves visible in the smoke, but that was a question for later, when I was on my own with them.

"Based on what you said about Gordon meeting people to collect debts, I'm going to search his house shortly. We found a notebook on him listing people who we think owe him money. No doubt we'll find a stash in his house."

"Tell him about the safe," Lily said.

I gave her a stare. I was sure O'Malley could find it without me.

O'Malley rubbed his eyes. "I'll walk you home."

I opened my mouth to refuse, then thought better of it. It was the middle of the night, after all. And while the murderer was no longer at large, I didn't want to go home alone.

———

In the morning, I still opened my tearoom, even though I had only slept for a couple of hours. It had taken me a long time to get to sleep.

I told Carole, Emma, and Alan what had happened, and they were shocked.

"You poor thing. That's terrible. You go home, Trinity. We can run things," Carole insisted.

Alan nodded. "I've picked things up quickly, haven't I? I'm sure we'll manage. If not, we can ring you."

"I feel bad leaving you all to it, though."

I looked at Alan and felt a wave of tiredness. It wasn't

unpleasant. It was as though I felt everything would be all right.

"All right, but if you need me for any reason, call me."

They all promised they would.

I was woken by the doorbell hours later. I half expected O'Malley, but to my surprise it was Holly's friend Izzy. She was the jeweller I'd commissioned to create the replica of the enchanted moonstone ring.

She proudly handed me a ring box. "All done."

I opened the box. "Oh my, it's perfect." It was exactly like the ring in the museum.

Izzy smiled. "I'm very proud of it. It could be the identical twin of the museum ring."

"Yes."

"Is it for you, or is it a present?"

I couldn't tell her the truth. "Um, a present. For a friend."

"Must be a good friend. And I can't say I blame them. It is gorgeous. Simple, yet striking."

When Izzy had gone, I put on the ring. It fitted perfectly.

Mr Collingwood inspected it. "It's an exact match."

"Yes, but how will we get the keys to the cabinet and swap the rings without anyone knowing?"

Mr Collingwood smiled. "Well, we've been talking, and we have a plan."

"You do?"

"Of course. All you need to do is get into the museum, and we'll do the rest."

I didn't like the sound of that. "I want to know how we're going to swap them. I'm not sure I trust you."

"There's no need to worry," said Mr. Wickers, which did worry me even more. "We've been over and over it, and we've worked out a foolproof scheme. Don't you concern your pretty little head about it."

My eyes narrowed. "Explain everything, or I'm not going."

Mr Wickers sighed. "So suspicious."

"I want to know what I'm expected to do. That isn't too much to ask."

Mr Wickers puffed himself up. "First of all, we will sweep the museum to check for other visitors."

Lady Camilla interrupted. "You will need to go near to closing time so that it is less likely other people will be there. Once we have done that, you will enter the museum and pay the entry fee."

"Wearing the replica ring on your finger," added Mr Wickers.

Lady Camilla continued. "You stay on the ground floor and browse the exhibits. Mr Collingwood will keep watch near the desk and check that the keys to the display cabinets are in the correct place."

Mr. Collingwood cleared his throat. "Then I will trip the electricity, which will halt the CCTV. When the volunteer on the front desk goes to the fuse box to try and work out why the electricity has turned off, you will take the keys from the front desk and go up to the first floor. Then you will unlock the cabinet and switch the rings, and lock it again. You will then go downstairs and replace the keys on the front desk."

I thought this over. It actually sounded like a decent plan. "One question. Are you sure you can blow the electrics, Mr Collingwood?"

He grinned and bowed. "Of course, madam. I have done it before."

I looked at the duplicate ring on my finger. It sounded simple.

CHAPTER 34

I decided to take the bull by the horns and get the switch over and done with, so I went to the museum late that afternoon with the replica ring on my finger. On the wall behind the front desk hung the museum keys. There were at least twelve sets, so I browsed the exhibits, and then when I was out of earshot from the volunteer on the desk, instructed Mr Collingwood to check the labels and find the correct key.

He floated off, and a minute later came back. "The correct key is on the bottom row, third from the left. The label is red."

"Bottom row, third from the left. Red label," I repeated, trying to imprint it in my memory.

"We're good to go!" said Mr Wickers nearby, and Mr Collingwood disappeared through a wall, presumably to the fuse box.

I moved to another display, this time slightly closer to the desk, and waited for something to happen.

And I waited. After what seemed a very long time, I checked my watch. Mr Wickers was nearby, chatting with Mr Darby. "Go and see what's taking him so long," I whispered.

They dissipated, returning a short time later.

"He's having a spot of bother with the electric box," said

Mr Wickers. "It's a newer model, and therefore more resistant to ghostly interference. He apologises for the delay."

I sighed. This wasn't going to plan, and we'd only just started.

I stared at the display case, eyeing the keys hanging behind the desk, every so often.

Eventually, the lights flickered and went out. I could still see, of course, as it was daytime, but the room darkened, and a TV playing a documentary about Sidmouth switched off.

"Oh dear, have the electrics blown?" I asked the volunteer.

He looked around, seeming rather surprised. "Yes, it appears so. I'll go and take a look. Back in a jiffy." He shuffled out from behind the desk and went through a door into a back corridor.

As soon as he had gone, I made my move. My heart pounded as I crept behind the desk. I had to remind myself that I was helping the ghosts and it wasn't stealing. Not really. It was replacing.

I reached for the bottom row and started counting. First, second … third? Or was that fourth? It was red wasn't it? But there was two that were red. My brain froze, the numbers jumbling in my head. I grabbed one at random, my fingers fumbling.

I checked the label. My dyslexia meant it took longer than others to read "Basement Storage".

Wrong key.

My pulse thundered in my ears as I shoved it back on to the hook, muttering under my breath, "Bottom row, third from the left. Third! Get it together." This time I forced myself to focus, counting slowly and deliberately. One … two … three. "First Floor Cabinets".

Finally.

I clutched the key ring tightly as I rushed upstairs, my legs trembling. When I got to the cabinet, all the ghosts except Mr Collingwood were waiting.

There were several keys on the ring. I tried the first: it didn't fit. Nor did the second.

"Come *on*..." I said in frustration. "Warn me if someone comes."

"Everyone is downstairs," said Mr Darby morosely.

I chose another key, but fumbled the bunch, and they clattered on the wooden floor.

"Oh, nasty," said Mr Wickers, making a face.

I picked up the keys and chose one at random. It slid into the lock and the cabinet opened. "Thank goodness!"

I was about to reach for the ring when the lights came back on. I jumped.

"Yo ho ho!"

I clutched my heart, then realised it was just the mannequin dressed up as Black-Eye Elmore. The motion sensor must have been activated. Then I looked up at the CCTV camera. The red light was on.

"Tell Mr Collingwood to trip the electrics again!" I muttered.

Mr Wickers floated through the floor, and a moment later the lights went off again.

I slipped off the replica ring and reached for the real one. Before I could grab it, the ring lifted itself toward the turquoise one on my hand.

I snatched it, quickly switching the replica in its place, shut the cabinet, and locked it.

I'd done it.

I gazed into the cabinet. No one would ever know the ring there now wasn't the real one.

Lily somersaulted in the air. "Yippeee! Well done, Trinity!"

"Yes, bravo!" exclaimed Lady Camilla. "Very commendable."

Mr Collingwood appeared. "You have it?"

"She has!" Lily said.

I looked down at the keys in my hand. "I must put these

back. Mr Collingwood, I need you to trip the electricity one more time, but wait until I'm downstairs."

He gave a small bow, then disappeared.

When I reached the ground floor, the volunteer was back behind the counter. He didn't seem to have noticed any keys were missing. I tried not to catch his eye as the room went dark.

"For goodness' sake!" he said, and went out, shaking his head.

I slipped behind the counter and put the keys back on their hook. Then went straight home.

I barely looked at the new ring in my hand until I was inside the house, with the door locked behind me. We had the enchanted moonstone ring.

I held out my hand and looked at the ring. The stone on top seemed to swirl.

The ghosts gathered around, gazing at it, too.

"It still has that pull to the turquoise ring," I said. "It's like a magnet pulling them together. What do you think that means?"

"Deep magic," Lady Camilla said, sternly.

I sighed. "Now, we need to find a direct descendant of Black-Eye Elmore. And then all we have to do is to persuade them to present the enchanted moonstone to the ghost that guards the map at the Volunteer Inn.

"Hmm," said Lady Camilla. "That will be an interesting conversation."

"I'm sure it will," I replied. "But it's a problem for another day."

I went to my bedroom and placed the ring inside my jewellery box.

CHAPTER 35

The last day of the festival passed by in a blur, and I'd agreed to meet O'Malley to watch the evening torch-light procession which closed the festival. It was one of the most anticipated events, famous for miles around because of the hundreds of people carrying flaming torches through the town, then onto the beach.

I'd arranged to meet O'Malley on the esplanade. I found him looking out to sea, studying the fading sun. He was in dark jeans and a T-shirt. An unusually casual look.

"Hello," I said.

He turned to face me. "Hello, yourself."

"Enjoying the view?"

He smiled. "I am now."

I felt my face burning.

It was already busy. People were milling around, some eating ice creams, some with trays of fish and chips.

"Where do you think is the best place to watch the procession?' he asked.

"It's been a long time since I saw it, but if we go towards the other end of the seafront, we'll be able to see more. Especially when the people with torches go onto the beach.

"They end up on the beach?"

"Yes, and then there's fireworks."

We started to stroll along the esplanade, the ghosts floating in front of us.

"How was Gordon before he was carted off to prison?" I asked.

O'Malley smiled. "What you mean is, did he get over the strange visions he had when he tried to kill you?"

I didn't say anything, just smiled back at him.

"Well, he confessed to everything, then begged for a priest, to whom he unburdened his soul and pleaded for forgiveness."

"That should make for an easy court case."

"There is that. As my grandmother used to say, 'Confession may lighten the soul, but it doesn't undo the deeds.'"

"Very true. You mention your grandmother a lot. Were you close?"

"We were. She was a fine woman."

"When did she pass away?"

"A couple of years ago now. I miss her every day."

We reached near the end of the esplanade.

"I think the best place to watch is about here," I said, and we stopped.

It wasn't long before the procession began. The soft boom of drums echoed through the air, growing louder with each beat. In the distance, the glow of torches flickered, weaving like fireflies in the twilight. As the procession neared, the sounds of fiddles and pipes joined the rhythm, their tunes mingling with the drumbeat. Dancers spun and stepped in time, their movements adding life to the music. A flood of torchbearers followed, creating a shimmering river of light that seemed to flow along the esplanade.

It was magical.

A few moments later, the first firework exploded in the

sky, tinting the sea with a brilliant burst of colour. The fireworks continued, growing louder and brighter.

O'Malley turned to me, the fireworks reflecting in his eyes. Then he leaned in and gently kissed me. "About time, don't you think?" he said, softly.

I laughed. "Yes. About time."

I spotted the ghosts all gazing up at the fireworks. All except Lily, who was watching O'Malley and me with a wide grin.

———

When I got home, I closed the door behind me and leaned against it for a moment. The house was quiet, except for the faint hum of the fridge in the kitchen. My cheeks still felt warm from the kiss.

Wentworth appeared almost immediately, padding into the hallway with a soft meow. He rubbed against my legs. "Hello, you." I bent down to scratch his head. He purred loudly, his eyes blinking up at me as if to say, *Where have you been?*

The ghosts had left me alone for the moment, though I suspected Lily was somewhere nearby, ready to start the commentary. I kicked off my shoes and went into the kitchen for a glass of water. Wentworth followed, his paws barely making a sound on the floor. As I set my glass down, he leapt gracefully onto the counter, watching me with a tilt of his head.

"Were you lonely?" I asked him.

He meowed in return as though answering my question with a yes.

The fireworks and procession had been stunning, but the day had drained me, and I felt an overwhelming tiredness as I climbed the stairs to my bedroom. Wentworth trotted after me, ever the shadow.

Once inside, I turned on the bedside lamp and began my nightly routine. I brushed my hair out, tied it loosely at the nape of my neck, and changed into my pyjamas. As I folded my clothes, my eyes drifted to the jewellery box sitting on my dresser.

The enchanted moonstone ring.

We'd done it – I'd done it. I went over and opened the box and there it lay among my necklaces, earrings, rings, and bracelets.

I picked it up and wondered whether to keep it safe or if I should wear it all the time.

Still holding the ring, I got into bed, and Wentworth jumped on, then settled in his usual spot at the end.

"Are you just going to stare at it, or actually put it on?" Lily's voice broke the silence, startling me.

I looked over to see her floating near the wardrobe.

"I wasn't staring," I said, defensively.

"Yes, you were." She floated closer, her eyes sparkling. "You've been dying to try it on."

The surface of the ring seemed to shimmer faintly, then got stronger as though alive. I hesitated for a moment, running my finger along its edge.

"It's like it wants you to put it on," Lily said.

I glanced down at the turquoise ring on my hand, then slipped the moonstone on to the finger beside it. It slid on easily, fitting as though it had always belonged there.

Wentworth sat up suddenly, his ears twitching.

For a moment, all was still. The room felt different somehow, as though the air had thickened.

Then a voice broke the silence. "Thank you, madam. I have been most eager for you to place the ring on your finger."

I looked across the room;, my heart leapt into my throat. Standing in the middle of the room was a ghost I had never seen before.

. . .

The End.

ACKNOWLEDGMENTS

T hanks to Liz Hedgecock, my editor and to my proofreader, Paula.

If you want to find out more about Jane Austen's visit to Sidmouth, you can download a fact sheet about it by signing up to my newsletter as well as a recipe for Devon Apple Cake:

www.suzybussell.com/tearoom

Book 3 in the series Riptides, Rivalries and Rigor Mortis is available to pre-order now.

ALSO BY THE SAME AUTHOR:

Exeter Mysteries Series:

Exe Marks the Spot Book 1

A disappearance. A murder. Two mysteries connected.

Meet Angus Darrow, straight-laced, ex-police detective, turned private investigator. He's hired to find a missing vulnerable young man whose parents are convinced he's been co-erced into something bad.

But in order to try and find the boy, technophobe Angus needs to recruit Charlotte Lockwood, a brilliant but unpredictable cyber security expert.

They quickly discover they need each other more than they realise.

With her technical knowledge and his investigation skills, will they uncover the mystery of the missing boy?

www.ingramcontent.com/pod-product-compliance
Lightning Source LLC
Chambersburg PA
CBHW060603190726
48283CB00003B/1139